Tales in the City

Volume III

Adapted into Short Film

Ukiyoto Publishing

All global publishing rights are held by

Ukiyoto Publishing

Published in 2022

Content Copyright © Ukiyoto
ISBN 9789360169299

All rights reserved.
No part of this publication may be reproduced, transmitted, or stored in a retrieval system, in any form by any means, electronic, mechanical, photocopying, recording or otherwise, without the prior permission of the publisher.

The moral rights of the author have been asserted.

This is a work of fiction. Names, characters, businesses, places, events, locales, and incidents are either the products of the author's imagination or used in a fictitious manner. Any resemblance to actual persons, living or dead, or actual events is purely coincidental.

This book is sold subject to the condition that it shall not by way of trade or otherwise, be lent, resold, hired out or otherwise circulated, without the publisher's prior consent, in any form of binding or cover other than that in which it is published.

Contents

Short Story by Dr. Alokparna Das	1
Short Story by Purnima Dixit	7
Short Story by Piyush Pratik Mohanty	20
Short Story and Poems by Valerie Blue Claveria	27
Short Story by Leslie Riola	84
Short Story by Charles Tomeldan	110
Short Story by Satabdi Saha	130
Short Story by Dante Villanueva Aguilar	149
Short Story by Kuntala Bhattacharya	171
Short Story by Taniya Briana	191
About the Authors	*195*

Short Story by Dr. Alokparna Das

Familiar Faces

It had become a routine: The office car that dropped her home after a night shift at a national daily took this Central Delhi route around 2:30 am every night. Sumita used to see men, women and children – mostly from the migrant labour force – sleeping on the pavements close to the iconic India Gate. Some had a blanket or a bed-sheet to cover themselves, while others were stretching on bare concrete. Since she saw them every day, the people had started looking familiar. The scene outside the car was straight out of T.S. Eliot's poem, 'Rhapsody on a Windy Night', where the narrator wanders around city streets till 4:30 am. A common sight in any big city that is dependent on these so called outsiders. She had seen similar sights at Kolkata and Mumbai.

Now that the entire place had been dug up to build and rebuild the Central Vista, sand mounds and deep trenches had made it difficult for those, who, till recently, found a refuge in concrete pathways during night, to come across a shelter under the sky here. It was strange, thought Sumita, the city didn't offer a place called home to those who beautified and developed it.

The huge heaps of sand reminded her of January 2001. She was in Gujarat, working for a newspaper, when the massive earthquake hit the region on the Republic Day. Sumita had seen high-rise buildings in Ahmedabad collapse like houses of cards and turn into heaps of sand. The horror was firmly etched in her memory. Despite the natural calamity, however, she didn't want to immediately return to her hometown, Delhi. But finally, unable to find a proper accommodation, Sumita returned home, and also took up another job.

The months after the earthquake had been tough. Portions of the building where she stayed had been declared unsafe. The aftershocks had forced people in the colony to sleep in the open. Every night as she returned home from her office, she would find people asleep on the floor of the community hall. They would keep a space right next to the door for her. No one would occupy that place. And as she sat down on the floor to retire for the day, someone or the other would call out: "Are you back from work Sumita *ben* (Gujarati for sister)?" It was almost as if she had been missed during the last headcount of the day. It was a touching moment. She was the only one in that colony who was living away from family. Sumita wasn't social. And there was no reason why she should be missed. Yet, the people there – most of whom she knew only by face and not name – seemed relieved to see her back. These were the same people who had frowned at her coming home past midnight. "Why can't you journalists finish your work within a reasonable time?" asked one of her neighbours. Sumita had found it very annoying, but patiently answered, "We work till late so that you can read the latest news in your morning newspaper." The neighbour shook her head in disapproval. For Sumita, it was difficult to understand this strange behaviour. She was appreciative of the same neighbour when a young woman started staying at their house prior to her wedding with the eldest son of the family. "Bhawna is trying to ascertain if she would be able to adjust with our family after her marriage," the neighbour had told her. "That's quite progressive," remarked Sumita's mother who had come visiting. A would-be daughter-in-law trying to determine whether or not the in-laws were agreeable people was fine, but for a working woman like Sumita, coming home late was met with displeasure. The earthquake, however, had erased those disapprovals. Her neighbours were suddenly appreciative of the fact that she was visiting victims and earthquake-hit remote areas and writing about them. "It was through the write-up that your newspaper published that I got to know that my cousins in Bhavnagar were safe and spending their nights in a truck," said one neighbour.

It's been more than 20 years since Sumita had left Ahmedabad, but the city hadn't left her. The old city's narrow lanes, the houses in the Pol area, the Pushtimarg shrines that appeared like *havelis*, the exquisitely carved Jain *derasars*, the calm ambience of Sarkhej, the medieval stepwell at Adalaj, and the late night trips to Manek Chowk to enjoy street food – it was easy to recall the smells and flavours of the city.

She also missed Sajjad and Renuka, her friends in the city who lived in Kalupur area.

She had called them immediately after the riots rocked Gujarat in 2002. Sajjad and Renuka were all set to get married that year and move to Mumbai, where Sajjad was to start his restaurant with Renuka as a partner. Their parents had been next-door neighbours for generations. Though the families were initially shocked to know that Sajjad and Renuka were in love, they had given their consent without much fuss. After all, they all lived as one big family. The riots and the politics of hatred that followed had turned their lives upside down. One of Renuka's cousin had been killed in Godhra and her relatives didn't want Renuka to marry Sajjad. Renuka had called Sumita. "I don't know how to tackle this volatile situation," she had said. And then a month later, a former colleague messaged Sumita: "Sajjad is missing, so is Renuka."

There was no news of either Renuka or Sajjad during the last two decades. How could two people just disappear?

Sumita's thoughts were disturbed by her co-passenger. Sayanti, her young colleague, was showing her photos of her sister's engagement. She had just returned from Kolkata. "We celebrated the occasion at a newly opened restaurant at Salt Lake. Look at the décor: the walls have visuals of some very beautiful monuments, particularly from Gujarat. My sister is getting married to a Gujarati businessman in Kolkata. The other day you told me about your stay in Gujarat;

perhaps you can recognise these heritage buildings. Sumita took a closer look. One wall had the visual of the Swaminarayan temple at Kalupur. Two people were standing in front of the wall, the man, wearing a toque – the white and pleated chef's cap – looked very familiar. "That's Samir, he is running the place in partnership with my would-be brother-in-law; that pretty woman next to him is his wife Rukhsar," Sayanti told her.

Making the picture bigger cleared all her doubts. Sumita asked for the restaurant's address. "The next time I am in Kolkata, I will definitely visit this place. The place and people look both interesting and familiar. Thank you Sayanti, you have refreshed my memories of Ahmedabad and perhaps also helped find long-lost friends," she told Sayanti.

Short Story by Purnima Dixit

Love is Not Blind

"Life takes us by surprise and orders us to move toward the unknown, even when we don't want to and when we think we don't need to." — Paulo Coelho

Ranvijay has just reached Shimla, after finalising Jeet's operation scheduled next week in Delhi, but here he sees Jeet sitting with his feet up on the lounge chair, his hands folded and face grumpy, he was about to ask Jeet about his opinion, if he is fine with a new nurse, as Dr. Mathur was supposed to send the replacement, but his wife Supriya prevented him talking to Jeet.

"Ran, we need someone experienced to deal with Jeet's post-operation next week. Saachi is just a young nurse. Lets go ahead with the new nurse coming today. This week, Jeet will get used to the new one.

But still the nagging feeling not leaving Ranvijay's mind, as far as he knew Jeet was coping well with Saanchi, the young nurse assigned to him, she was longest to survive with this grumpy, irritated rude man, who at one point changed 6 nurses in one single month. Sometimes he wonders how Saanchi managed to survive a whole long year. As Jeet's brother, he is now used to his attitude and mood changes since his accident, but Saachi was a calm and composed nurse, who handled Jeet very well.

It was Jeet's decision who wanted to move away from Delhi, city life and wanted to recuperate at their hometown, Palampur, in Shimla. Dr Mathur, was kind and understanding enough to appoint full time caretakers, who came back running, not able to handle Jeet's attitude and rudeness, until Saachi was appointed.

***

Two years ago, Ranvijay didn't know if he should thank the doctor for saving his younger brother whom he raised like his son after their parents passed away, or if he should curse the same doctor as Jeet has lost his vision. Despite the severity of the accident, still, Jeet managed to defeat death, with his leg fractured in two places, and dislocation of shoulder muscle, all these were not very complicated as the doctor already operated and put a cast on, more shocking and disturbing was glass prism of car windows and rear-view mirror shattered and entered his eyes damaging both of them. Looking at Jeet all plastered and bandaged broke his heart, his body injuries will heal with time as he is still young and healthy, but what worried him more, was how he was going to handle Jeet and console him as a blind man. Though it's temporary, Doctor has confirmed he can regain vision after the transplant, but it can't happen very soon, not unless Jeet gets fully recovered and is medically fit to undergo surgery.

***

The accident drastically changed Jeet's life, once a full-of-life person, always an achiever, who was just running fast steps towards success, growing his business, and making his parents and brother proud. Life threw him down in just one flick. Growing up in boarding school, Jeet had been the boy who was self-sufficient since childhood but now is dependent on others even for personal chores. Jeet was always a bright student excelling in studies, sports...living an active lifestyle, enjoying as an adult, occasional clubbing, partying, having his share of flings in college life, by his thirties turned into an efficient and successful businessman running a chain of hotels, climbing success ladder very early, making a name for himself. Jeet knows his brother is trying hard to motivate him, to keep him strong. His brother is trying everything he can, to the point where he feels guilty about being a burden on him. There are moments when he is scared of this darkness—everything was dark, just pitch dark, and he felt suffocated and breathless as if confined into a small box, though his legs are out of the cast now, his movement is still hampered, they still need strength and support to regain his previous dexterity, he still needs the support of stick to move around, he is confident with the regular exercise he will be able to walk like past, but with his eyes gone, sometimes he thought it would be much better if he had died in the accident. He doesn't care about increasing pain, after every physio session, he is confident he will get his stride back with time but due to his blindness, the solitude, the darkness, and the loneliness around it just suffocate him, every single minute takes him back to the memory of the accident. The nightmares of that fateful night don't let him sleep—all his efforts to fight and survive seem worthless because of the darkness around. Ranvijay is making arrangements for his eye transplant faster, he is updating him regularly but he has to get back his physical strength, but more often this darkness frightens him, angers him, depresses him, what if the transplant fails, will he have to live with this darkness forever. He hates the feeling that people can take advantage of him, he is vulnerable at this moment, he is fighting a war, every single day is like a battle for him, where he can't walk properly, he cannot dress without help, he can't eat properly, without being guided. To add to everything, it is dark all around as dark as it can be and he hates this darkness. He would not have regretted if his hands or legs would have gone, but his eyes he regrets the most. He has spent sleepless nights thinking that he will no longer be able to see the things which he loved most, he would not be able to see people whom he loves the most, and he will no longer be able to be the same confident person he was. He was in his favourite place, where he was born and brought up, he has always loved hills, snows, trekking, camping, every season. He made sure to take out time for his Shimla visits, in spite of his busy schedules. He had always been in control of his life.

But now, his life changed, and is changing and he has no control over it. He is at the mercy of others, he hates to be pitied, to sympathise—he doesn't want such a dark life, where he can't be in control of his own life. He has stopped dreaming, what's the point of dreaming in the dark? But amidst all this darkness, he saw a light of hope, when he met Saanchi, she is the one who inspires him to start dreaming again. Saanchi the young nurse who has been taking care of him for the past 1 year... in fact as a nurse and his caretaker she was the most patient one with him, she dealt calmly with him since the very first day. He has given a tough time to his previous caretakers and they ran away, giving up in a few days.

***

He also realises he is not an easy man to handle given his moods. She used to scold him when warranted and appreciated when he did something on his own. Also always motivated him, cheered him up with her lame jokes, and silly banters, she always managed to pull him out of his depressing moods. He smiled a bit remembering her non-stop chattering, and she never felt daunted by his unfailingly grumpy, rude and mood swings throughout the day. They occasionally ended up arguing with Saachi ignoring him for a maximum of two minutes, and soon she wud be back to her chirpy behaviour.

It was she who had seen him spending sleepless nights, dull mornings, and his breakdowns. She had always consoled him.

He still regrets saying "he hates her" the very first month she had joined her duties, and he has thrown away medicines, feeling they are useless.

"What's the point of taking them? I can't even stand properly, can't get up from bed, do things which I wish to. Even if I want to do something, even a simple task of just getting up, it hurts like hell! Don't know if I will ever be able to live like I used to. And you always are grinning and all cheery like a fool, everyone is healthy and full of life! I hate to see you so happy, with nothing to worry about. While I lie here like a rotting vegetable, just with darkness around while everyone watches everything. My career which I worked so hard for is in ruins, my life in tatters."

Even surprisingly, he broke down crying. Days of mental anguish had taken a toll on him and he felt completely failed by his inability to cope with the mental stress and the compounded darkness around being cooped up in a room.

Later when he calmed down, Saachi took him to the rooftop, making it their daily routine after dinner for the "Star Talk" session as he named it, where they used to sit and talk for hours, she shared her childhood stories, her pranks, her antics, her dreams. He still cracks up the memory of her sharing her dream, that she wanted to be an actor, she even mimicked actress voices. Her soft sweet calming voice was the first thing that attracted him. No wonder he so smoothly fell in love with her.

"Love." Yes, love. He has no doubts about it that he has developed feelings for a girl whom he has never seen, he wished he could see what she looks like, he has this picture of her in his mind on the basis on her limited touches, smell, her voice and of course her strict lectures, her senseless banter, her laughter. He might not see visions around, but he can see himself as a man falling in love with a girl he has never seen.

Many times, he was tempted to ask Ranvijay about how Saanchi looked, but then he did not want to shatter the image he had in mind. He doesn't even know how old she is, never asked her but he did calculate how old she can be, she had told him the number of years she has been working, when she passed out from college, etc, so he can guess her age. He doesn't know if she was in a relationship or not but he knows she is not married as he could feel her fingers which were warm and soft, and there were no rings on her fingers.

***

Jeet's heart was beating with excitement when he heard the doorbell at the designated time. He couldn't see the time, but it must be 10 am. Saachi was never late, but he was shocked when he was greeted by a strange voice. He couldn't fail to recognize Saanchi's voice. He wondered what was wrong with her, was she still shy? Or was she hurt because of yesterday's events? But her reactions didn't say so...

Just the thought of yesterday had brought a smile to his face, if he is honest with himself, it's the first time he genuinely smiled after the accident.

He had not intentionally planned anything yesterday he had just held her hand and they were just having their usual "Star Talk" session when he randomly shared his thought with Saanchi, that he wants to know her more.

Jeet: I have a picture of yours in my mind, even in this darkness I can see you.

Saanchi thought he was just joking, so she pulled back her hand.

Saanchi: I don't know what picture you have of me, but I might look very different from your imagination.

Jeet: You have a sweet voice, soft touch, and warmth, I guess you might have a sweet smile and love nature too.

As he gazed into her eyes, Saanchi felt his eyes bored into hers, for a moment she felt as if he could see her, as his fingers brushed her cheek and he lowered his face to take her lips ... and there was no stopping.

A nagging voice in his mind did try to reason with him that he should stop himself, but he didn't know why he didn't attempt to stop himself. Neither did Saachi, she did let him go all the way.

***

The memories of last night will stay with him forever. The feel and the touch is engraved in his heart and mind. It was magic, a multi-coloured explosion in slow motion. It was like knowing her layer by layer, the fumbling fingers undressing her, shivering fingers touching him. His strong body, her lean body in bed, his roughness, his gentleness, her shyness, passion. Tears and emotions—together their hunger had built to greed that had to be satisfied the moment he began to make love to her.

How he wished he could see her expressions, her emotions, her smile, her shyness. He could still feel the softness and warmth of her hands when he held them while proposing to her.

Jeet: I do not know if you have anyone in your life, but to me, you gave me strength and encouragement. I know you are paid to take care of your patients, it is part of your job, and for you, I am just one of your patients, but you have touched my heart and I would like to start dreaming again with you, marry you, as you are my strength. Will you accept me as your husband, lover, father of your children? I don't care how you look, but still, I have a desire to see you as the first person when I get my vision back. That will be a new beginning for me, and I want to start this new journey with you. And yes, you can think about the proposal till then, but I want your answer to my question on that day itself.

***

She checked her watch. It was already 5 pm. Her shift was over. She needed to rush back home; her little brother must be waiting. She wound up her work and briefed Nisha, her follow-up nurse, about critical patients. Then she heard a voice asking for her name, the voice she can recognize even in her sleep. A voice she had been avoiding for the past two weeks and not giving in to the temptation to run into his arms and melt in a puddle. She literally pulled Nisha on her seat and removed her name badge, asking her to be Saanchi for a while. Then she went back to the ward.

Nisha: I thought your shift was over.

Before she could complete her sentence, she saw a gentleman in front of her asking for Saanchi, carrying a beautiful bunch of baby pink roses. She did introduce herself as Saanchi and said thank you for the flowers.

Jeet: I can see your badge is missing and it seems pulled out in a hurry. Never mind, I know you are not Saanchi, but do tell your friend that nothing is wrong with my hearing. I was blind, not deaf.

Nisha was about to apologise.

Jeet: No need to defend your friend. I do not know how she looks but I do know her touch and her voice. My ears know her and my body knows her, enough for me to find her out.

He left smilingly, waving bye to Nisha.

***

It's been two weeks since Jeet had his successful transplant. Saanchi was with Dr. Mathur throughout the process. And after he regained his vision, she made sure she stayed away from Jeet, and now with her duty in the emergency ward, she had not enough time to focus on Jeet. She didn't know why she was running away from Jeet. For some strange reason, somewhere down her heart she knew Jeet was genuine in his confession and he must have liked her. But she feared if it was just one of Jeet's emotional phases and he wasn't serious about the proposal. To be very honest, she had been overwhelmed by how close she had been with Jeet and how genuine he was in his confession. Maybe it was just her fear of knowing that Jeet's sister-in-law didn't like her, or it was just her guilt of breaking the rules of the nurse-patient relationship, she would be blamed for taking advantage of an emotionally vulnerable person.

Saanchi sighed in relief as she peeked from the window and saw the car leaving. Now she can safely come out from her place of hiding, after changing her dress, she was about to pass through the main door when she felt a pull on her wrist and felt pushed against the pillar.

"You thought you could fool me like this? If you forgot, I did get my eyesight back, I can see things around."

Saanchi shockingly looked at Jeet. She thought she saw the car leaving. How could he still be here?

Jeet smirked. "Don't need to be too surprised, the driver just left as Bhai needed him back urgently. I am still here! Now can I know why you are hiding away from me, or precisely running away from me? If you forgot I can repeat what I had said earlier: 'Pyaar ki jeet hoti hai, yeh sab jaante hai, aur mere pyaar ki jeet tumhari haan se hogi, aur Saanchi ka Jeet ho chuka hai, yeh sabko batana hai.' (Everyone knows love always wins, and my love will win with your acceptance as Saanchi has won over Jeet.)

He pulled her in for a soul-stirring kiss.

"I never needed eyes to see that you are beside me. Even in the darkness I saw a bright future with you. So I would officially want you in my life to assure me that you are near me and will always be with me, taking care of me, as my wife."

He swiftly pushed the diamond ring onto her finger.

"Sorry, had flowers for you too, but gave them to Nisha!" he joked.

Short Story by
Piyush Pratik Mohanty

Tale of Traffic

It was a sunny day. Sunil was in a hurry. He was already late for his office so he was working like a machine; doing all the stuff precisely at the speed of light. He lived alone, prepared his lunch, took a bath and did all other necessary household chores. Sunil, 25, is a bachelor living alone in a peaceful yet busy city. He landed on his very first job last month. Coming back, he locked himself in and finished his household works and without delaying any further he locked the door of the house and sat on his bike and started his journey towards his office. He was already late, nearly 15 minutes of official working hours were already gone.

Sweta, 23, lived with her parents in the same city. A student, pursuing her engineering degree from a nearby institute. As someone has famously quoted, Indians are always on time but late, so following the same notion Sweta too was late for her classes. Moreover it was Monday, the day everyone wants to kill themselves for their misery; the day full of high intensity of misery. She took out her scooter and started her journey towards her destination i.e. her college.

Sunil and Sweta lived nearly fifteen blocks away from each other in the same society but as the houses are located far off they never had met each other until this very day of Monday. Sunil, already in a hurry, was looking at the traffic lights to turn green so that he could fly off to his workplace. Exactly at the same time, Sweta, on her scooter was waiting too at the traffic junction, beside Sunil. Just like a normal boy's attitude, Sunil too took a glance of Sweta but exactly at the same time, lights turned green and Sunil started his bike and started moving but in an unbalancing manner and as a result of it he fell off. Moreover, it wasn't the worst part, the worst part was that he took down Sweta too with himself rather he fell on Sweta's scooter and it's result was that she too got heavily pulled by the Earth's gravitational force.

Now, the accident happened in India, so there has to be drama associated with it along with the live audience and the same did happen. Sweta, showing her female power, got aggressive and started howling beautiful words at Sunil but on the other way, Sunil who was very new to his job wanted to get off without any further delay so he apologized to her but Sweta wasn't in a mood to let her go. She continued firing words at her faster than a bullet leaving the gun. Within a minute, Sunil's threshold of taking in broke and he started yelling too. Thanks to the traffic police personnel who came in like the UN and ensured peace prevailed between them. Within 5 minutes both of them went off to their respective places, she gave him a stare for a fraction of a minute before leaving. Both of them left for their respective hectic workplaces. Making the already depressing Monday more melancholic.

Monday went by, and came the next day with new opportunities and desires, this is what people say to pseudo-motivate someone but this ain't the truth feels Sunil as he knows Monday to Friday he have to work up like a machine, hear it out from the bosses and return back home with no one around to comfort him. So he was losing hope steadily but then there's always room for hope in every second of life.

Sweta was a more light hearted, live-in-the-moment kind of girl. She did whatever she felt was good not thinking twice before committing or doing something; in short she was carefree. But still, today's stressful life takes a toll on you. No matter if you are an overthinker or not, no matter if you are carefree or careful, it will take down every kind and the same was happening with her too. The gut-wrenching pain of going to study something she was never interested in was doing the talking for her.

Two days went by, then came the day which brought truce to their fight. It was early in the morning and both of them, ready to move to their respective places, went off in their two wheelers. The traffic junction had a red light and it was déjà vu all over again as Sweta was exactly beside Sunil and the unique thing was that no one else was standing there in their side of traffic, it was just them. Sunil looked laterally towards her in a bewildered way, thinking to initiate an apology or conversation and complimenting him,

Sweta too wanted to apologize him for her words but both of them were lacking the push and suddenly both of them realized they were looking at each other, hence got uncomfortable and looked in different directions with a smile; a smile full of blush and awkwardness. Soon the red light turned green and this time no déjà vu happened of the incident and they took off to their places. Boys get the feelings first and this time the same happened. Sunil while riding his bike started thinking about her face and felt that he was getting this adrenaline rush thinking about her, hence he was starting to crush on her. Sweta though wanted to apologize didn't think much of this stuff and to be fair she wasn't thinking at all.

With new hope came the next day. Sunil started his bike exactly at the time Sweta came out of her house and crossed his house which implies he was trying to see her in the traffic again today. Again both of them were by each other's side. Getting this rush of dopamine, Sunil wanted to have a conversation with her but soon his luck ran out and this time red turned green within a couple of minutes of their waiting and Sweta just flew off though this time she noticed him staring at her and also the awkward smile. She was amused at first but then she didn't think much of it and ignored it. Sunil on the other hand was disheartened and angry at the lights and his luck.

Similarly, the next day, he prayed to God for a ten minutes red light so that he can talk to the woman he has a crush on. God heard his prayers but there was a slight problem i.e. she was standing in the middle of three or four other vehicles. Looking at this, he exhaled a lot of carbon dioxide but he didn't want to lose, so he made his way up to her by quarreling and rambling with others and finally he got near her. He also saw that there was one third of thirty minutes left for the red light to turn green so he knew this was his chance. He said, "Hi! Sorry for that day madam. It was really my fault." She replied, "Even I am sorry for my behavior."

Both of them keep smiling looking at each other, blushing really hard. No one was uttering a single word and there was absolute silence. Smiles were speaking a thousand words though. Sometimes silence helps connect with someone more efficiently. The lights turned green soon and both of them started moving, greeting each other bye. Sunil was already in his magical world but this time it hit Sweta as she felt a spark too. While driving towards her college she was just thinking about his smile and apparently the same was the scene with Sunil. The melancholic workdays weren't melancholic anymore. Both of them started feeling it.

Both of them wanted to talk to each other but lack of time made it possible to converse only in the traffic. So mutually without talking to each other beforehand, they both came exactly at the same time to the traffic junction. Slowly those five to ten minutes felt like an hour or more than that for them as they both started to talk to each other more transparently, conversing about their fears, stress and happy stuff.

Slowly and steadily the traffic red light became their happy place. For the first time, one can actually say that the red light of traffic actually came in handy for some people. Nearly three months passed like that. They both enjoyed their company. Evidently, both of them wanted to take this to the next level. So finally, after an epoch they planned to meet outside where there won't be any involvement of traffic lights and vehicles.

They just really hit off very well. Two years passed by like that, Sweta graduated and got a job, Sunil was doing his management and was almost on the verge of passing out. Things started to change when both of them realized that Sweta had to leave the city for her job. Everything was changing except their love for each other. After 6 months, Sunil shifted to her city and got a job there and finally decided to live together. Nearly after a couple of years, Sunil took her to the same traffic junction in their home city and proposed to her. Nothing to think more about, they lived happily ever after.

This depicts that love can find a way anyhow. Let it be traffic lights or any other place where, if something is meant to happen then it will definitely happen without any hesitation and doubt.

Short Story and Poems by Valerie Blue Claveria

Trail of Blood

For 31 years now, I have relied on my Baptist conviction for my daily sustenance of strength.

Sure, I changed when I suddenly gave up on my chastity principle on August 23, 2014 but my old self still remains intact, pure but carnal, ideal but pragmatic, both spiritual and worldly.

I have lived with myself for 31 years now. At times, I cannot reconcile or put into words the chain of events that happened to my life. But in this journal, I will try to relive my life and thus, tell my story.

The journal will be subdivided into parts based on my tattoos. First, is the rice bundle acquired in Buscalan, Kalinga by Apo Whang-od in December 2015. Second, would be the Tetelestai Bogdan Dr. Albert Bela Marosi, Ph. D. recently tattooed on December 22 2016 and lastly, the two Little Prince tattoos acquired in January 2017.

I. Rice bundle-Panyat

II. Tetelestai

III. The Little Prince

This book is a form of closure to my past as I start another chapter this 2017. I just turned 31 last March 24, 2017 and that child would read this book or compilation, thus the title 'Trail of Blood'. It will chronicle a past that is controversial, draining, adventurous and worth relieving, written in three chapters, Panyat-Your ancestors watching over you for protection, Tetelestai means "It is finished", Bogdan means gift of life, Dr. Albert Bela Marosi, Ph. D., and of course, The Little Prince.

I. Panyat-Rice Bundle

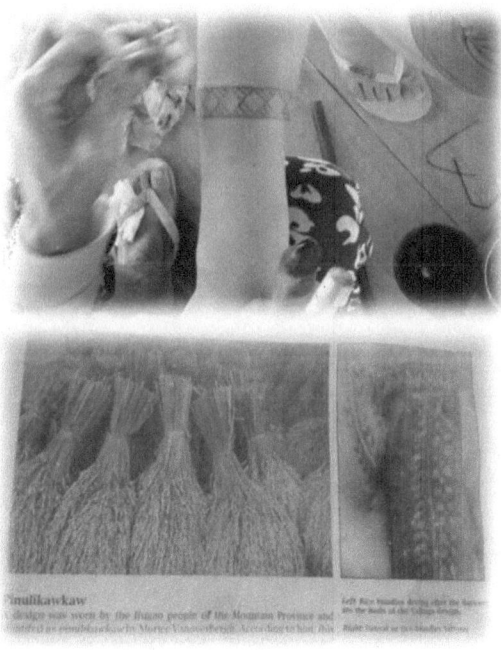

II. Tetelestai

III. The Little Prince

In order to learn how it is to be a woman we must start with the one who made her—Elizabeth Elliot, Let Me Be a Woman

I.   PANYAT - is a version of the mata which means your ancestors are watching over you for protection.

My Lolo Olivas Claveria married Lola Maria Pawig and they had six children. My father was the second eldest however my Tito Baylon Claveria was ambushed in 1986 so my Dad Binsin Pawig Claveria assumed as firstborn. My mom Corazon Luban Dam-at on the other hand was the eldest among a brood of six and she has an A+ strong-willed personality. Early on, she showed leadership capabilities graduating as Valedictorian and a constant achiever in school. My Lolo Andrew Dam-at (Lolo Anyo) was a former Barangay Captain during the Marcos Regime (thus holding a little influence) and he married Anita Luban and they had six children.

In 1983, my Lolo Anyo was ambushed. In 2012, my Lola Maria died of breast cancer. In 2013, my eldest sister Atty. Xandred Anne Dam-at Claveria died in a vehicular traffic accident.

I have four more siblings. Next to me is Vincent George Dam-at Claveria, married to Odette Balalang Carmoc with a 6 years old daughter in the name of Sabina Roviezon. Vincent or BJ for short also has a previous relation that bore fruit; his firstborn is named Khriz Daniel Claveria. She is now 9 years old living in Palawan with her mother named Gracelle Lopez y Dimayuga. Vincent is a licensed Criminologist and is presently connected with the Philippine National Police under the Intelligence Group Division.

My next sibling is my sister Vinazon Dam-at Claveria, her name is a combination of my parents' name, Vinz from Vincent or Binsin, and Azon from Corazon. She is a registered nurse and is presently working for the Department of Health under the Nurse for Deployment Program (NDP) in Pudtol, Apayao.

The fourth sibling is Dexter Dam-at Claveria who is married to Joana Cabico in October 2015 and he is a Hotel and Restaurant Management Graduate (HRM). He has a prior relation with PO1 Analyn Arugay and they had a son named Xednyle Xander, named after my deceased sister Xandred Anne. Xednyle is now 2 years old.

Lastly, my youngest sibling Angelic Dam-at Claveria who is currently single and was a product of UP Diliman Industrial Engineering graduate in 2014. She is now currently working in Sydney, Australia.

Let me just insert some whereabouts about my late sister Attorney Xandred Anne or Twinkle here. She is the firstborn among a brood of six. She was born on October 25, 1984 and died at 28 years of age on April 24, 2013. She was single and a promising young lawyer when she met her end. She loved two men, Engineer Darwin Andres, a classmate in Elementary and Highschool and a steady boyfriend since first year College, in 2001 up to 2010. In 2010, ate Twinkle developed feelings with Sir Jerome Lacambra, the former Chief of Staff of then Congressman Butzy Cayaba Bulut, Jr. when she was still working as Chief of Staff of the late Governor Elias Kirtug Bulut, Sr.

So much for my background, let me introduce myself. By the time I am writing this journal, I am now officially 31 and still single. I loved two men, Attorney Raymund Erwin M. Pizarro, a former law school classmate in the University of the Cordillera's Bachelor of Laws and Letters batch 2010 (UC-LLB) Section A. The second love would be, PSUPT Dexter Baguan Ollaging, the former Deputy Police/Program Directorate for Administration (DPDA) of Apayao PPO in 2014. We met at work when I was still connected with PNP- Apayao as Fingerprint Examiner or Non-Uniformed Personnel in 2014.

At present, I am employed in the Department of Social Welfare and Development as Project Development Officer II (PDO II) under the Sustainable Livelihood Program. I am also in the process of completing my last academic units at Cagayan State University (CSU) for the Doctor of Public Administration (DPA) Program. Hopefully, after completing the academic units this year, I still need to take my Comprehensive Examination in order to be allowed to start my Dissertation before I can finally graduate.

Overall, my employment history usually adds color to my life because for the record, I have worked in four government agencies so far and these are (1) LGU-Apayao/Provincial Capitol of Apayao (2) Department of Trade and Industry- Cordillera Administrative Region (DTI-CAR) (3) Philippine National Police-Apayao (PNP-Apayao) (4) Department of Social Welfare and Development (DSWD FO2). Amidst all these, I also managed to experience working in 3 private institutions namely (1) Banco De Oro, Unibank, (2) Teletech and (3) Sutherland.

Needless to mention, there are many loves past and present and this is just the tip of the iceberg.

The next chapter, Tetelestai, will be more interesting.

Tetelestai

Tetelstai means "It is finished." Or "The debt has been paid in full." Bogdan means "Gift of Life." Dr. Bela Albert Marosi is a scientist I met on Tinder in December 2016. We chatted briefly until we finally said our goodbyes. I will be inserting his resume below. By the way Bogdan is the Mongolian name of his child.

Dr Béla Albert Marosi, PhD

Dr Béla Albert Marosi, international researcher and academician from Rumania ,Europe currently working as Professor in Mongolia International, University under Dept. of Biotechnology and Food Science. He lead the department and supervise students specially Lab experiment, research and field bas scientific experiment. He did his PhD Molecular Biology Centre, Institute for Interdisciplinary Experimental Research, "Babes-Bolyai" University, Cluj-Napoca. The PhD project was acrried out under the scientific supervision of Prof. Univ. Dr. Octavian Popescu. The title of the PhD thesis is: Molecular markers for amphibian and reptilian population genetics. Course of Evolutionary Genomics of Natural Populations at the Biology Education Centre, Uppsala University, Sweden. He has published number of international jurnal paper and Book chapter. He dedicated to work internationally on the field of Micro biology , Human and Animal health, molecular biology and genetics, water qualty Management Research etc. Major Publications are follows; 1.Béla A. Marosi; Karen M. Kiemnec-Tyburczy; Ioan V. Ghira; Tibor Sos; Octavian Popescu. 2014. Identification and characterization of major histocompatibility complex class IIB alleles from three species of European ranid frogs. Molecular Biology research Communications (MBRC) 3/4: 215-222; 2.Marosi AB, Sos T, Ghira IV, Popescu O. 2013. COI Based Phylogeography and Intraspecific Genetic Variation of Rana dalmatina Populations in the Vicinity of the Carpathians. GERMAN JOURNAL OF ZOOLOGY RESEARCH (GJZR) 1: 7-16, 3.Marosi AB, Zinenko OI, Ghira IV, Crnobrnja-Isailović J, Lymberakis P, Sós T, Popescu O. 2012. Molecular data confirm recent fluctuations of northern border of dice snake (Natrix tessellata) range in Eastern Europe. North-Western Journal of Zoology 8(2): 374-37, 4.Marosi A. B., Ghira I. V., Sós T., Popescu O. 2011. Identification of partial MHC class II B exon 2 sequences in two closely related snake species: Natrix tessellata and Natrix natrix. Herpetologica Romanica 5: 1-6.

Source: google.com

April 14, 2017 Friday (HOLY WEEK)

TETELESTAI - It is finished.

Now let us move on to the subject of my heart. Let me tell you a long story. And unlike the first chapter which I initially drafted in a notebook, this chapter will be encoded directly in my laptop and will be sent via my email for backup purposes. I hope that I can articulate the events logically and present a factual narrative.

I met Dr. Albert Bela Marosi in December 2016 but before him there were many men and I can only account this story as personal views.

I was born a Bible Baptist believer because my parents were pioneer members of the San Gabriel Bible Baptist Church which was founded in 1984—the year my sister Xandred Anne was born. I received the Lord Jesus Christ as my personal Lord and Savior in the summer of 1998. In my assessment, although I only learned about the temperament book by Dr. Tim and Beverly La Haye in 2004 or the end of my first year in college, I was born a choleric. When I say that I was born choleric, I mean to say that I was born with a conviction. Early on, upon realizing that I have the capacity to attract the opposite sex because of my gifted bosom, I decided that I have to guard my chastity so that on the night of my wedding day, I would be the gift for my husband. This was an ideal I had because when I watched the interview of President Corazon Aquino, she said that their first kiss with her husband the late Benigno Aquino was during their wedding. This was later reinforced in the form of attending summer camps from Pastor

Tuazon of the Metropolitan Baptist Church about Love, Courtship and Marriage that ideally, it should be long courtship or getting to know, short engagement and marriage. This is primarily due to avoid the couple engaging in pre-marital sex. I held on to this conviction for so long.

On a few notes, I was also a born evangelist or shall I say born-soul winner. I often say that it is my gift for I always had it in me to share the word of God in public or even in my best friend's home. I remembered that in elementary days, I had the passion to share to Ate Margaret Baloran, Marifourth Baloran's (one of my elementary best friends and neighbor in Soldiers Hill) eldest sister, and Ate Margaret would ask me back "Ibig mong sabihin Bluebelle, after magkasala ng tao, hingi lang sya ng tawad, okay na ulit." I cannot recall how I answered that question back in the days but I do know that whenever I share the word of God, I had this gutsy, awesome confidence, a feeling of becoming invincible—like there is an inner power inside that is empowering. God it's so awesome, the feeling that anything is possible.

So now, let's transition to the love angle. In 1992, I was a transferee student from Tuguegarao East Central School in grade 1 to Caggay-Tanza Elementary School in grade 2. Being a transferee student makes one popular. I remembered that all the boys in my class are giddy and one very gutsy boy named Greg Paolo Pagalilauan kissed me in the cheek abruptly probably with the teasing of his fellow boys. That would be remembered as my first kiss. But my first crush ought to be mentioned. His name is John Christopher Maltu and we like to play "takbukan" for I was a good runner back in the days. My female friends especially Roselean Ford Dasayon or Queen liked to play "Ten-Twenty" wherein we have to jump in the roped-like rubber band and the length of the rubber band would go higher for every correct step. Well that was before I transferred to SPED.

In grade 3, I was section B with my teacher Mrs. Maltu. But I was selected to join the pupils that would take the qualifying examination for the first batch of Special Education (SPED) section in Caggay. Luckily, I passed and I would just like to point out one story that is worth mentioning. I did not know that the section A was already taking spelling lessons as a review for the upcoming test. One of the words to be spelled is government which I spelled without the "n" because it was pronounced as "government. " The classmate who corrected me was Robertson Magora and boy, was he not only smart but good looking as well. All in all, I passed the SPED test that consisted of I think over 150 spelling test and 1 essay—the essay was pre-memorized to us and mine was entitled—My Orquidarium—written by my mother. When I became SPED, the class consisted only of 29 students with only five boys.

Being in the SPED section has its perks and privileges because most of the time, we were asked to join extracurricular activities which gives me much pleasure and my mother fully encourages us to attend because according to her, she did not have the same privileges growing up as a child. Mama's motto would be "Anak, you cannot buy experience." I joined the Girl Scouts of the Philippines when I was in grade four. Street dancing, Science fairs, Press conferences, Folk dances during programs, name it in elementary days, I have joined most of the extracurricular activities and it was mostly fun and socialization. The Caggay-Tanza Elementary School is part of the East Central District.

In grade 5, I had a crush or infatuation with Robertson Magora but at that time, he also had a relationship with Ate Florabelle Joves, the Valedictorian of grade 6. Anyhow, in grade 5, I was imagining that he would lather my back skin with lotion while I was sweeping the fallen leaves in our sector. That's why it is called infatuation. In grade 6, several boys in the class had a crush on me, for one, there was Ethan. And second there was a nice decent, good looking, good physique guy from section B named Rocky Pagirigan and he gave me red roses and a card in 1998 valentine's days, and thus I told myself that when he continues to court me until third year of high school, I would say my yes to him as my first boyfriend on our Junior Prom. I was not new to attraction then because at an early age, I was courted and I had quite a few if not several crushes.

My fun filled life and sunny disposition continued in high school. During the first day of school at Cagayan National High School (CNHS), I proceeded to wear a very revealing outfit, a blue flowered sleeveless, blue mini skirt and white rubber shoes. The outfit I almost forgot had it not been for the incident that would happen next.

In my first year of high school, being the sociable sanguine that I was reared, I became friends with my classmates instantly. I voted for Carmeline Eclar to become our muse due to her long and curly eyelashes. But the person I became close to in terms of opposite sex is Lindon Richie Basco—I treated him at that time as a gay friend and I am so happy when he was around.

In 2000 when I was in second year of high school, I visited with my mom on a summer vacation in Quezon City and we stayed in the house of then Congressman Elias K. Bulut. I remembered that I was wearing a pink blouse that day but then after our stroll in the park, because we used the DTI-issued car/red plate, I was so disturbed that I couldn't sleep. I do remember that I was sensitive to the noise of the cars passing by the village or private subdivision that I can only account today as a feeling of paranoia. I would hear the closing of car doors and I thought that someone was following me. I thought that maybe the person saw me inside the mall when I was wearing a brown and mocha gap, above the knee dress. The feeling that I was being followed never left me. So much so that came June 2000, after I found out my new section, meaning I was promoted in Section 1, Regular Section, one morning during a flag ceremony, I closed my eyes, and felt my heart. After I opened my eyes, I immediately imagined and declared that Byron Jake Lasam, the third year student who is vying for Salutatorian, was the one who caused the feeling. Meaning I thought that he was responsible or that he was actually the person who was following me. It was so awkward and humiliating because from June-October 2000, I did everything to follow this guy— chasing him and confronting him in the walls of the main building. The main memory that I hold on to pinpointing him as the culprit was the time when I saw him and he saw me, during the first day of classes in first year in front of the ESF Building. The scandal became a controversy when I couldn't concentrate on my studies and flunked my entire $y=mx+b$ math workbooks from Mrs. Ascano's class. I flunked nearly all my subjects— failed in all my exams, I would get stomach cramps and regular bowel movements in the morning (despite desperately trying to read the Bible to give me sanity). It was a case of sleepless nights and paranoia or mental disturbance. I felt so betrayed by my emotions because for someone who has no care about the world to suddenly be subjected to that type of weird attraction was beyond imaginable. Hence, I thought that in order to end the feeling, I would chase him and express my feelings until it ends or stops. So drastic was my measure that I also began calling their landline number in the wee hours of the morning resulting in her mother's getting a high blood. To make matters worse, one night, I heard men having conversations inside my head, sounds like drunk neighbors who were laughing and sharing some stories. I went out of the house to find peace in the mountain, this was around midnight and I did not know then that I had my monthly period and I had stains in my white shorts. Luckily, Queen's house was near the rice fields and when my family, especially Tito Mina/Pilbert Claveria tried to look for me, at least, Tita Nanette Dasayon, the mother of Queen already came to the rescue.

My mother patiently waited for me and fetched me in the car everyday so as to avoid chasing Byron. My sister Twinkle who was working in the Guidance Counselor asked the guidance counselor to excuse my behavior and my mother putting it into writing as excusing my confused behavior as part of growing up or adolescence or coping with puberty.

That was the year 2000. In 2002 during the J.S. Prom, I had unrealistic expectations that Byron would be my first dance and it did not happen. The JS Prom was held in the People's Gymnasium so Rocky Pagirigan who is probably in the lower section is nowhere to be found. By this time, I completely forgot about Rocky Pagirigan and my oath during my grade six. In short, no first dance for me, and it was my first lesson about expectations. In summer of 2002, I went on a vacation in my sister Twinkle's apartment and I met his dormmate, I forgot the name. By June that year, I was in fourth year and things about my love life were doing great because I pretended to be June, who is studying in Centro Escolar University. Ate's dormmate and I became text mates because the 3310 cell phone was introduced in 2000 and texting became pretty common.

Let's fast forward my college years and I will not tell you one by one the boring details of the story. I had a blast in college years at the University of the Philippines. Baguio is full of organizations—the lifeblood of my academic years. There is the Baguio Residence Hall (BREHA) which is a social group in itself, Campus Alliance for Dedicated and Unified Action (CADUA) for political organization, Alpha Phi Omega for my Fraternity and Sorority (APO), UP-ACE for academic org, UP Reel for Journalism students, PAGTA or Program for Indigenous People for Indigenous group and most especially, Campus Crusade for Christ (CCC) for religious organization. I spent most of my time in APO and CCC.

For matters of the heart, I had a crush on my History teacher Mike Ang in first year, James Salvador from Alpha Phi Omega in second year, Lemuel Pelagio from Campus Crusade for Christ in third year and Nimreh Calde, my Political Science teacher in fourth year.

In 2008 and moving forward, the same cycle of attraction took place, a thing that I was not able to recover or conquer.

There was an almost suicidal type of feeling, a feeling of death and helplessness and abandonment, a feeling of flight and struggle and a time where I just cry from the soul and write journals and cry and cry and cry because my soul at these times is in anguish and tremendous pain. It is almost like I cannot get myself to accept a partner. It is so difficult for me to even start dealing with the person because of so much pain and crying that is from the soul—deep and soul wrenching cries is how I would describe it.

So in my first employment in July 2008 I met Albert Tuala our Area Operations and I had a crush on him. I resigned in April 2009. In May 2009, I transferred to LGU Apayao and I met Sherwin Agudelo, the son of the former Mayor of Kabugao, Apayao. He was married and I knew that before I became involved with him, I needed to resign. In June 2010, I enrolled myself in UC-LLB and there I met, Raymund Erwin M. Pizarro. He was the class president or mayor of section A and I developed feelings for him in November 2010. In March of 2011, after a heart wrenching incident where my parents decided to come to Baguio and take me home after I was reported to be disturbing my dorm mates, or causing trouble in my apartment in slaughterhouse, I was diagnosed with Schizophrenia, specifically Auditory Hallucination.

I will elaborate further on the sickness in chapter 3: the Little Prince. For now, let me finish the story. In June 2014, I met PSUPT Dexter Baguan Ollaging.

Due to this incident, I resigned in February 2015. Finally in December 2016, after being healed from the Ollaging fiasco, I was ready to open my heart again and I met Dr. Albert Bela Marosi. This time, I told myself, it's high time to mark or symbolize my journey by getting inked with the letterings of "Tetelestai": meaning "it is finished" with the name of the last person I ought to fear love from being included in the tattoo.

All this sounded easier on paper than it was with the actual experience. Now, we can segue to REMP, my sickness or my last perfume—for he was the last person I was with before I acquired the sickness.

The Little Prince

Oct. 10, 2016

You are afraid That death will take

Me, in my sleep And you are checking To see if I'm still alive, Through my dreams.

After the long saga of lost loves that I have experienced, I need to talk about "it"---my sickness. First, let me take a deep breath and read what has been revealed so far. The time and date in my laptop reads April 14, 2017, at 10:52 PM. I have read the transcript of what I have written so far, and some of the paragraphs in chapter 2 are long, so now let's talk about my sickness.

The Little Prince is simply defined as -THE ORGASM

In March 2011, I was diagnosed with Schizophrenia specifically Auditory Hallucination. I do not know what my sickness is but to describe how I am feeling, it was as if I had created an imaginary friend and I called or referred to that friend as Raymund or Poy for short, Poy being the nickname of Raymund.

[I just need to compose my thoughts so I will take a quick break] We resume at 11:43 PM; 4/14/2017

I scramble to find words to describe or express my ordeal.

In a nutshell, I finished reading the book entitled "The Little Prince" by Antoine De Saint Exupery in September 2014— after the Ollaging incident.

The moral of the story is when fox told the Little Prince the secret and that is "What is Essential is Invisible to the Eye." So to begin this, let's begin with the ending. The story about the tale of my so-called guarding the chastity ended on that fateful night in August 23, 2014. We were as usual tied at work with the Performance Governance System (PGS) that Friday night. I was wearing a pink brassiere, lavender panty, Gray Aeropostale shirt and diamond patterned black and white puruntong shorts. At 9:00 PM, there was a need for the PGS team to download a file on the internet at Luna Municipal Police Station. Sir Ollaging volunteered to drive me to the station and my mood that day was so light and I was beaming with happiness. In the beginning, when I first sat on the chair in the front seat, he asked if I brought with me a usb and upon discerning that the gigabytes might not be enough, he offered to give me a backup usb. After that, he started the engine and everything was fine. He drove the car out from the Camp Allan Gate then down the cemented road of Barangay San Francisco, there was a space where no houses went down that road and he started kissing me. The French kiss was unexpected and it was good. He then kissed me in other parts and hell break loose. The rest was history.

Now let's rewind a little bit and backtrack to 2010. In 2010, I met Sherwin Agudelo, a married man with 1 kid and I decided that I would give up my career in LGU-Apayao in order to study law in UC-LLB. I did not know then that love was a relentless pursuit and that it would be inevitable to meet a new one. But I was a little suspicious. Having been acquainted with a lot of attractions in the past—I thought I had this coming. But I reasoned that I came to Baguio to study and I will be focused and goal-oriented in following my purpose.

Raymund Erwin M. Pizarro was the talkative classmate at the back of my chair in the second row. He was talking to Jo-anne Ventigan. He was talking about his sister who graduated Cum Laude in Nursing and had it not been to her, he would not realize that he already spent 7 years in college in UP Manila as a Political Science student. He was sharing his stories and the usual during the first day of classes.

Let's cut the chase and proceed to the highlights. In October 2010, I had a date with two of my classmates (a female and a male)—the boy said that "Gusto ko sana ligawan si Val kaso may bumabakod naman na sa kanya." You see I sort of liked this guy so I retorted "Sino, si Pizarro, hindi ah, platonic lang kami noon."

The thought bothered me and when I went home and took my semester break, I became uneasy. I spent my new year in Tuguegarao City and went back to Baguio in 2011. Around this time, I already knew that I failed my Constitutional Law 1 class with Dr. Liceralde—a subject to which he got the highest grade in all of first years. In January of 2011, I was failing my grade and then decided to move or transfer houses with them and some other classmates in order to cope with my failing grades. In February 2011, I gave up my boarding house in Sandico St. and moved in with them in the five bedroom apartment in Slaughterhouse. My other housemates were Regina Sandajan, Jo-anne Ventigan, Raymund Pizarro and the guy I was talking about to whom I had a date in October 2010—I forgot his name. He is currently connected in a government agency and is a working student like me who previously taught English as Second Language (ESL) to Korean students in the International Masters of Educational Centre (IMEC). Regine, Jo-anne and Raymund were all full time law students and are quite excelling in class.

So anyhow, I do not know why but my parents intervened—I later learned that Raymund Pizarro texted my Ate Twinkle—that apparently I was disturbing my classmates who wanted to review for exams and so they had to get me out and bring me home.

A spiral of events happened in 2011. First, I developed an imaginary friend I talked to which I refer to as "Raymund." Second, I thought that I was the Holy Spirit and Jesus Christ was coming back and that I needed to declare some things. This was all in March 2011 after my parents took me home.

Things continued happening and I started getting a job at Teletech MOA, Pasay. My sister was also taking her Bar Exams Review that time and I became connected with the company from September 2011 to December 2011. I only resigned because my Lola Maria was diagnosed with breast cancer so I had to go back to the province and spend time with her. When I went home, she was so thin and the cancer had already spread in her (I cannot recall if left breast or right breast) breast leaving a big lump of tumor which my cousins Glenbee and Jessa Carolyn alternately clean in the morning. My main role during those days was to sing her Baptist hymnals because it soothes her spirits and helped relieve the excruciating pain. I would often hear her pray to God to please let her die, but apparently she endured for almost 3 months and she finally died in March 2012.

During Lola Maria's wake, the result of the BAR was released and it was a bittersweet celebration for we are grieving her death but at the same time, the good news has come that my Ate Twinkle is now a lawyer.

During these times, I also started touching myself and would find pleasure in the clitoris—my favorite part of the body next to the mind. Here I would have torrents and waves of orgasms which accelerated to greater and greater heights of extreme pleasure.

Anyhow, my sister Xandred successfully graced the signing of the roll of Attorneys in May 2012 and so after the death of Lola Maria, I received a call from Sutherland to attend an interview for a Business Processing Office (BPO) or call center as Customer Care Representative (CSR) so again, I packed my bags in May and headed to Manila. The process was easy and smooth sailing and I was employed under the Ebay United Kingdom account under Security Services from June 2012-December 2012. In January 2013, I yearned to land another job so I contacted Judy Guanzon and it was very timely that one of her clients, Pastor Woo is in need of a private tutor for his granddaughter named Sharon, she was then studying in a normal Filipino Baptist school and in her elementary years.

To make the long story short, I managed to worked there while struggling to finish my Masters in Public Administration, because at that time, I regularly go home in Tuguegarao on weekends to finish the last of my academic units in Cagayan State University-Master in Public Administration (MPA) program, the course that I started in the second semester of 2008 when I was still connected with Banco De Oro and left unfinished in 2010 when I had to leave LGU-Apayao to study law in UC.

In March 2013, after 3 months of staying with Pastor Woo, living and eating together with them, staying in Sharon's room, something horrible happened. One lunch break, Teacher Judy walked down the road to buy lunch for her. She was then stabbed by a random stranger who aimed to snatch her cellphone. The perpetrator used a screwdriver to stab teacher Judy. The incident impressed on me that I needed to resign.

True enough, something bad is bound to happen, because surprise of all surprises, on a normal Friday afternoon in April 19, 2013, we received a call at home in Soldier's Hill that my sister Xandred encountered a vehicular traffic accident on their way home from Luna, Apayao to Tuguegarao City. The accident happened at around 4:00 PM in Alcala, Amulung, just a few minutes away from Tuguegarao City proper.

There were four passengers that afternoon, all female. My Ate Twinkle was the driver, cousin Dinalyn Rumbaua was seated beside her in the front row, and at the back seat were 2 nurses Chams and my sister Vinazon Claveria. The 3 of them only suffered minor abrasions whereas my sister Twinkle suffered the most from the impact with broken bones in the legs, and internal hemorrhage in her internal organs. She has to undergo major operations right away. While our 3 patients were whisked in a private room in Saint Paul Hospital, Ate Twinkle was hospitalized in the SICU for 5 days until she finally passed away on April 24, 2013.

It was the most shocking and most devastating event by far and losing her meant losing someone so precious and dear to me. She was also planning to settle down with Engineer Darwin Andres that year after his recent breakup with Sir Jerome Lacambra.

Past forward to 2014 when I met Dexter Baguan Ollaging. And in December 2016, Dr. Albert Bela Marosi—the two persons were previously introduced in chapter 2.

Why is it entitled "The Little Prince"- My Orgasm?

Well, (1) I still constantly talk to myself up to these days.

(2) I also continue to touch myself up to these days.

I still call "him" Poy or Raymund. The conversation is real. It's the layman's term or equivalent of talk therapy or self- talks—talking my thoughts aloud when I am alone in my room. The presence of another being, or when I am with someone else automatically stops this tendency.

I repeat. The presence of another being, or when I am with someone else automatically stops this tendency. It puts an end to the sickness. So I only tolerate it in the confines of my own room.

Well, that's it for the first three chapters. I wanted to put this story into writing to complete my healing stage and to flush it out of my system. There would be no need explaining my tattoos and my reasons for getting them. There will be more freedom and liberation and a clean slate of 2017, 31 years has dawned.

Done 1:11 AM; 4/15/2017

I Told the Stars About You: Adonis Ampongan

Last night, I told the stars about you.
I told them how you healed all my wounds,
And kissed all my worries goodnight.

I told the stars how
You are a kinsmen redeemer to me,
How God shaped your heart to be
Like King David-- a man after God's own heart.

I told the stars how you honored
My life held convictions,
How you gently eased me into
Unmasking my Impostor self,

And patiently removed the layer of my
Protective walls.
Last night, I told the stars that you are the sexiest man on earth,

Having shared to me intimacy,

And mostly demonstrating honesty.

And the stars laughed.

Yes, they are a great number of little bells that knew how to laugh.

And I know that for you,

Once you read it,

You can look at the stars and know

That they are wells

With rusty pulley.

All the stars will pour out fresh water

For you to drink.

Akin to the little prince, I will have five hundred million little bells and you shall have five hundred million springs of fresh water.

Last night, I told the stars about you. And they glistened.

Bugs Blue 06.18.21

Permission to post: Adonis Ampongan

June 13, 2021
At the 39th of my existence,
We have found ourselves
loving one another.

And we loved, and laughed,
We chatted and talked
for hours.

We played games, and
traded secrets.
We watched news,
And stayed up late.

She brought back the spark
in my eyes,
Her stories brought joy
to my heart.

His quietness, my peace
and gentle rest.
His smiles, my inspiration.
I dreamed of a love,

Long lasting and true.

I dreamed of a lover,
Wise and gentle.
It never occurred to us,
She/he is right there within my reach,
We had to wait two decades,
Before we were allowed to meet.
--Bugs Blue 06.13.21

Tetelestai

(The debt has been paid in full)

The night is wounding.
Where darkness, and shadows,
Where thieves of joy,
And deadly wounds,
Where mortal sins, envy, lust,
Wrath,
Dreams and visions,

They seek space,
They covet company,
They assert incidentals and by products,
And my soul flushes,
Sweat and tears of sorrow,
And surrender,

Countless denials,
Ripped and stolen joys,
And sunshine/s,

I would ask for ceasefire,
A quiet rest but they
Would not halt.
This tunnel.
This curtain of the deep
"D" which is slight
Depression I call
Momentary or "occasional blues".

They call out my name.
At dusk they come,
Always with shadows.

They weave songs and poems reserved only
For the brave hearts.
If you can call it that.

Perhaps we have a choice.
Perhaps mine is to sing lullabies of indignation,
And a bloody surrender of
Heartful woes.

The pain that cuts,
The memories of untold past,
Curses and sighs,
Forbidden truths.
My life is borrowed.

What is reality?
How beautiful is your mind?
How did God designed your heart?
You have stamped your story in red ink,
Genuinely mesmerizing, tho
Bordering neurotic.

Your journey shy in one bottle
Of cherished tears.
There is beauty and great pain in waiting.

Let the night wound, bleed, cut,
Strip you naked.
Until at last, the right of passage.
Where dawn ushers a bright new day,
Tetelestai (The debt has been paid in full).

June 10, 2021

An ongoing love affair with the moon

--To bugs and poy my imaginary friend

06.08.21
Ti Biag Ku

Kayat ku agsurat ti Ilokano
Uray nu dyak met nalaing agsau
Adut damdamag nga agkasar nak kanun
Kitan ta man ngarud ti biag ku

Nabiyag gak nga aldaw ket arapaap ku
Uray rabii agbarbara ti kapintas ken isim ti biag ku
Adda manang ku nga twinkle ket syak mek ti bluebelle nga ading na
Isuna't puso ken dallim ku

Kasasaat ti biyag di met impagarup
ti namnama
Pigmusay (en) ti pigsa idi pimanaw isuna
Besnag ken lapat inkabel babain da
Imparswa na nga biag isuna met lang nangala

Ti sabali nga lubong agduduma paricut ken danag
Aging aging ti agsawsagawising

Naliday ken madi ti ricna

Bayam impalubos ni Apu Agyamanak imbareng ku

(Baroque sorry. Patawarin. First time.)

Adut napasamak di met lang nagdanag

Ammuk nga han baybayan ni Apu

Ti agkabsat nga naisem dimet

Isut rugrugi ken isu arapaap ku

Uray nu maymaysa agtalik nga ti bulan ket agbalin aldaw, iti puso impaay na kinni manang ku, di nak agdudwa ti parabur mu Apu

--to Twinkle, Atty Xandred my first muse

We miss you Ate. Lab lab.

Love ading ubel.

06.07.21
To Bugs My Soul, My All
(BUGS My Bunny, Honey)

He uses music to seek the eternal,
Who does not know his own genuis.
Somewhere behind him is an ocean,
A spiritual journey borne of him alone.

Fear and love reside in his heart,
Strangers, passing by.
An epitome of a saint,
In countless ways special, tho human with contradicting tryst.

In a field of grass, he stands tall and golden,
Narrow leaves, parallel veins small inconspicuous flowers.
Much like his countless moods and shadows,
His silhouette dances with the shadow of the moon.

With my old loves, I would always say I am the sun and he is the moon that borrows energy from the sun.

I am earth and him being moon has an ongoing love affair with the ocean.

With my new love, he occupied the constellations,

Cause his spirit is deep and so is his passions.

To the mysteries that I cannot fathom, to the darkness that is his soul,

From the depths of his heart to the perspicuity of his intuition,

No longer sanctimonious just blessed beyond words.

05.29.21

Lapat

(orihinal na kathang isip, maaring di totoo)

May kwento ako sayo
Tungkol sa yo/sa inyo.
Alam mo bang bawat babae
Iba ibang mundo.
Bawat lalaki
Iisa lang ang mundo.

Kaming mga babae
Buhangin ng oras.
Kayong mga lalaki
Bitwuin ng mga tala.
Kayo na binhi ng buhay
Kami na lupang sisidlan.

Ganun tayo inukit
Ganun tayo mabubuhay.

At alam mo ba may isa pang secreto

Bawat matalinong babae alam ito.

Kayong mga lalaki

Iisa ang litid niyo.

Kaming mga babae

Pag nahanap mo ang sayo.

Parang isang bitwin

Na dating kayo,

Nagiisa sa mundo.

Sana'y naintindihan mo.

05.29.2021
Anino
(Pinagod mo ko/Sanayan lang to)

Natuto na akong...

Sariwain ang yong sugat.
Buhayin ang pait ng mga alat.
Namnamin ang buhay,
sa mapanlinlang na balat.

Damhin ang musikang salat.
Bigkasin ang talinghaga
ng tulang ngpapahiwatig.
Ng daang patungo sa sapat
Ngunit di tiyak na payapa.
Di magpapahinga,
Sa pagtupad ng pangarap,
Ng iyong malayong anino,
Aking kaulayaw na sa yo'y nakikipaglaro.

Pasilip ng isip.

Parinig ng pintig ng puso.
Marami na bang sekreto?
Sakin din yan ipapatago.

Baybayin ang dagat ng yong ulap.
Haplusin ang hanging sabik,
Sa himpapawid.
Maski sa panaginip,
Ibulong mo habang nakapikit.
Takipsilim ng gabi sayo patungo
Takipsilim sa umaga kami'y ngtatagpo.

Alam mo ba kung pano naging tayo?
Tinapos ko muna,
Ang natapos mo na.
Matagal na ngtatago,
Bumabalik sa yo.
Sa akin din naman yan galing,
Pinapatakas ko, pinapalaya.
Ang laging sambit at pangako,
Kilalanin mo pa sya,
Makikilala mo sya,
Makikilala mo ikaw,

Makikilala mo tayo.
Tatlo tayo. May kaulayaw.
May anino.

Walang sagot sa yong tanong,
Kundi isa pang tanong.
Bawat pintong binubuksan,
Nakapalakip sa isa pang pinto.
Diba't sinabi ko sayo?
Ano bang iniisip mo?
Ano bang nararamdaman mo?
Ako nga yan.
Walang iba.
Galing na yan sa akin,
Sa kabilang dako.

Natuto na akong magpalaya.
Tayo'y magtatagpo.
Akin din yan ipapatago.

05.29.21
Duyan, Alay At Atang Ko
(Para kay Bugs, aking katipan, aking kabiyak)

Araw araw namamatay
Nalulunod sa kalaliman
Nakatingin sa karimlan
Sa nakadadapang kasukilan

Madilim ang umaga
Mahaba ang gabi
Di lubos maunawaan
Pagdakal ng bagwis

Nglalaro sa karimlan
Dinuduyan ng kalungkutan
Inaagos ng dugo
Na sa lupa ay dumuduyan

Mga damdamin na may mata
Mga matang may pakpak ng hangin
Ngsisilbing atang

Alaala di masupil

Alay ka nya sa akin
Atang kita sa kanya
Duyan mo ko ngayon
Duyan din kita

Itong pagkaulila
Sinukat ng mga katha
Sa ating mga palad
Sinulat ang kanilang tala

Mukha ng pag-ibig
Di maabot ng rurok
Mababaw o di kaya walang kapantay
Nghahari sa puso

Hay dito na naman tayo
Balik sa dating panahon
Di na ba ngbabago
Inukit ng alaala

Sa kahulilip ng kahapon.

Tayong dinuduyan
Ikaw na aking atang
Ikaw na kanyang alay.

Bukas abangan mo
Susulat ako
Ng iyong mga anino
Aakuin ko para sayo.

Pahinga ka na kuya
Lilipas din lahat
Paggising mo ng umaga
May pag-asang hinaharap.

Sabi ko naman sayo
Babalik ka din sa mga yakap ko
Tiwala lang kay Bathala
Syang pasimuno.

Di bale pasasaan ba't tayoy magsasama
Di ka na magiisa
Pagibig na di mawawala
Duyan, alay at atang

Paulit ulit mang manligaw
Pasasaan ba't
Tahimik na mananahan.

Para sa aking kalaro sa isip

Ikaw na matagal ko ng kathang isip
Nakasama ng isang dekada
Simula noong ako'y nagsisimula pa
Musmos at inocente sa pag-ibig
Bago sa kamunduhan
Ligtas na katawan

Nakasama kita sa realidad at sa kahibangan
Sa lahat ng kalokohan
Sa bawat pagdapa at pagbangon
Sa bawat pagibig na di ngtatagal
Sa bawat maling karelasyon
Sa bawat iyak, sakit sa puso, at hapong katawan

Sa bawat bagong kagkatuto
Andyan ka sa loob ko, sa isip at sa puso at sa katawan, kabiyak ko parang iisa tayo

Sa pagkat ang totoo, ikay imahinasyon ko. Natatanging kathang isip. Kalaro sa isip.

At sa mahabang panahon, tayo'y tayo.

Madalas mali, madalas pareho. Pinagbiyak, magkasangga, hindi anino kundi ako sa loob ng ako. Isa pang pagkatao. Ako pero di ako.

Madalas kasalungat pero sa huli magkakasundo. Ang ako sa isip na tanging kathang isip ang kayang mangukit, humulma, magpakitang tao. Magkatawang tao na may ikaw sa loob ng ako na totoo.

Pano ba yan, nahanap ko na sya.

Maari bang ako'y lubayan mo na.

Patahimikin ang isip na matagal na napagod

Iniwasan ang lahat ng tukso na sa katawan ay nangahas sumubok.

Nahanap ko na sya.

O di naman kaya nahanap na nya ako.

Nahanap na namin ang isat isa.

Sa totoo lang kamukha mo sya.

Isang panaginip. May kalaro.

Madalas nililigawan sa kabilang dako.

Nalulungkot, ngtatanong, nakikipagusap.

Napakalalim. Tulad mo ring di ko maabot.

Madalas nakikita ko sarili ko sa kanya noong mga panahong tayo pa.

Walang pinagkaiba, ngayon tatlo na tayo.

Pano ba to. May ikaw at ako. At ngayon magkakaroon ng kami. Ikaw din ba sya. Maari ba kayong magisa. Upang ikay di magambala. At sa aming dalawa manahan ka.

Tapos na ang matagal na paghihintay.

Iindayog mo kami sa yong duyan

Patulugin, upang muli patuloy na managinip.

Aking kathang isip, kalaro sa isip, palayain mo ang aking pag-ibig.

Sapagka't kaming mgiisang dibdib. Pag-ibig na mapagpalaya humango ka. Sa mahimbing na tulog kami'y mananaginip ng aking sinta.

Mananaginip sa mundo ng aking kalaro.

Kathang isip, makakasama ka hanggat sa huli at sa pag-amin.

val@35

-to bugs and remp my imaginary friend

May 22, 2021

05.06.21

"It is in the the quiet crucible of your personal, private sufferings that your noblest dreams are born and God's greatest gifts are given in compensation for what you have been through."

-Wintley Phipps

05.06.21

Because he
is
before the
was
and is now
to be.
#Adonisium

It's Tough To Be A Teenager

Just Beginnings-2003 Articles

Second Semester
November 7, 2003 Friday Morning

When I turned 13, the world seems to be
Very welcoming
High school friends and beginner's luck, I think
Everything's working out smoothly
Turning 14, however, drastically altered almost
All things
The most crucial stage, they say, where puberty
And falling in love has a price to pay
And how can one forget, the age of 15
With big events like JS Prom, for sure, it will
Be unforgettable
But of course, there's this sweet 16 thing
When pressures from school nags a graduating

Man (student)

A quest that have its good and bad times

Good thing I learned so many things

And now that I'm 17, I realize it's all

Worth it.

Anticipation Turned Apprehension

I look forward for my debut…
But my parents do not seem to.
I am loving somebody…
Everybody knows he's intelligent, wealthy and handsome
But notwithstanding, so what?
I got my transcript…
Almost all my grades did not meet my
Expectations…
My anticipation turned apprehension.

College Life

Oh! How beautiful it is
But it's also distressing
Especially, like me, who have low grades but
At least it is passing and with the
Prestigious title: "University of the Philippines"
Plus, I have my friends, who, sure is one of
A kind and my families support, it's
All I ever wanted
The sembreak is too short, so now,
We're back again
Where studying is a never ending process,
This is all I have to say.

4:30 AM 11/7/2003

Short Story by Leslie Riola

Billionaire's Space Time Travel Love Affair

Prologue in the form of a poem:

Your love is like a gold, oh so malleable!

You can change your face and body, what is your label?

Your Obese Number II Body makes my heart in trouble

I can't get you off my mind, should I rebel?

A billionaire's son, you're in front of me over and over again

Tears fall in my eyes, I keep waiting in vain

Your true love is what I am asking for

Should I let you go, or ask God some more?

Prince and Princesses in the country surrounds me

But you're the only person who stands out truly

I am madly in love with you, how can I be free?

From this dramatic agenda, years have passed already.

Your Obese Number two body is magnetizing me in that temple

You're a Bear Polar, and I'm a Bipolar

How can words be so powerful that it hurts me even if I graduate with flying color?

Your Obese Number two body keeps me wondering if you're still in that grand temple.

You're always in my mind; I don't know how I can move on

Laughter and tears with you, I keep on looking at our picture on my phone

I want some clarity, peace, serenity

With you, my life is complete and truly happy

To the God above, I hope He would give me signs

Should I let go, or should I hold on to times

Times that you said and prayed over me

That you are my God's answered prayer, truly.

I miss you so much, how your big butt waves

When I call you Baby A, you will smile and have that pretty face

You look like a mascot, and then your eyes have tears

Whenever people call you fat, I hope we all know how you feel.

Smile from yesterday's failure,

Stories of today must prepare for the future

Life is a journey, one must enjoy

You are obese, you look like a mascot, but you are not a toy.

If I can paint your picture from my memory,

Would it be lovely?

Would my loneliness, be cured?

This journey of Billionaire space time travel, I hope I can endure.

My best friend is an owner of a shipping company

I don't want to end up in tragedy

I think God, wants me for Baby A

I hope God can ship my Billionaire's love for free.

We dine together at night,

I know you shed some light,

You are big and white,

You are truly a mighty knight.

Every single night were together

Your jokes are recorded together with our laughter

I am known by your brother

Because I am your brother's secretary and trader

Life gives problems while on top

If problems cover me like a blanket, I just want to take a nap

I hope the world will stop

When we walk hand on hand

You would open your gigantic umbrella

We would eat your favorite Nutella

I hope I would be your forever Bella

Through ups and downs, I am your fella'.

You are my angel

You teach me that you are here to protect, every single day

You are my angel

You taught me to trust and have faith in you come what may.

How can an angel teach me to cry so hard?
To wait for you, with no doubt
You are tall and stout
A person who makes me cry but laugh so loud.

Billionaires, princes and princesses surround me
Beauty queens, CEOs, and athletes advises me
Best of the best that's how people are defined
Being with them, I must be intellectually inclined.

I want to forget my yesterday
Move on, be the best for today
But things doesn't work that way
Love brings me back to Baby A.

I let you go and see what will happen
If you will come back again
You're mine forever
I'll be prepared for whatever it is going to happen.

You declare your journey in my life,
I didn't believe in you because there's much strife

All I have is pride

I will come back to you at the right time for a lifetime.

You own a TV Channel, I am a writer for a company

Do you think were just so lucky

To be the best in our chosen career and in terms of money

If were together again, we can be oh so happy!

I remember how you cheer how handsome you are and how pretty I am

You would be so happy stretching your arms all you want

Laugh with so much confidence, that's what you are

A friend, a lover someone who will be there for me forever

If we meet again, will you change your body type from obese to macho?

All my life I've been waiting for you, my life is in loco!

All my life, I've been preparing for you to be my life partner

I hope you go back to me, and stay with me forever.

Your boomerang love, taught me to have faith

Loving you, is what I will wait

We will eat your favorite chocolate date

Wines, Pasta, we'll share our dreams together until our hearts will no longer have a heart ache.

Your boomerang love is what makes me alive!

I release your affection, you promise me to have faith all my life

Willing to wait until *Deus-ex-machina or God-in- a-machine* happens!

No more reason to fail, but marriage for the both of us will just happen.

Time is wasted, waiting for you

Still waiting for signs, if I'm really meant for you

Making the best version of myself just for you

I will be waiting, for that obese guy who shares his life with me.

I

If you love someone, set him free. If he comes back, he's really meant for you. Like a boomerang, have faith because he will surely come back.

Engiel Airano Victorino was the first guy I learned to love simply because he stayed with me for four years of my life. Every single night, he's telling stories. Nights turn into months and into years. Engiel is a name given by his dad. Engiel because it's a word play from the two words Engineer and Angel. Engineer creates and fixes, and Angel protects. So he is a creator and a fixer and a protector in his family. He creates computer software, good music, literary artworks, films and he's a protector because he is good at kung fu and studied military science.

His lessons during his primary years were so advanced as compared to his peers because of tutors his parents hired. He is a billionaire, the unico hijo of the Victorino Family, a family who owns a Broadcasting Company in the Philippines that is aired even in different countries around the world. He can speak six languages- English, Filipino, German, French, Italian and Latin. He is a six footer and one inch guy, obese number II person, who always where white top and black pants. His cologne is the air freshener in the car. I don't know why he doesn't use colognes but he loves the smell of his car so much that the air freshener embraces the smell of his clothes and his skin. He is bubbly and cute probably because of his very pointed nose and white skin. If he is an animal, he will look like an elephant.-big and emotional. Call him fat and he will cry. He is a giant guy who always loves to play his IPAD when he is bored at things. He loves watching football and cheering for his team. He would sit beside me whenever he watches football. I don't understand football, but he was really happy watching football and cheering for his favorite team. I usually play with his man boobs, and he is so confidently happy because he is more macho than his peers who are also big and fat like him. I usually compare him with his Vice President in the Organization in the university who is a law student, and he laughs so hard, because for him he is oh so macho even though he is fat! If he is slim, surely, he won the genetic lottery. By winning the genetic lottery meaning, he has a very great combination of genes. Tall, handsome, pointed nose, a brain that is the crème of the crop—very good looking, very smart. We were only 19 years old when we were together. Happily, saying our family secrets together.

We met at the University of the Philippines Diliman. He was supposedly a graduate already during that time, but he had a failing grade in one of his subjects. FAILING GRADE! Would you imagine his first sister is a sumacomlaude of Philosophy and then she became a lawyer, then his brother is a double degree sumacomlaude of Religion and Music at Yale University? And look at what they've got, a young boy who keeps sleeping at his subjects, and who earned a failing grade despite the good example of his older sister and sister? He wanted to curse his teacher for his failing grade, because it was embarrassing that he will be the next in line to become the Chief Operating Officer of the Broadcasting Corporation. Maybe, he is really just a kid, that he thinks he is really smart and he never saw his shortcomings. He is the type of guy who can sleep in some of his classes and when the exams come, he would have a perfect score. Is it telepathy or is he just a gifted child?

He has lots of jokes whenever we are together. UP CBo, the name of our organization, always play together these two games- Dugtungan ng Kanta or Connecting Songs and Pinoy Henyo. Dugtungan ng Kanta is when the first person sings, whether it is two or three lines only, the last word must be the first word of the next player- and the game continues. For example,

Deanne Lozarie: Dr. Jones, Jones

Calling Dr. Jones

Wake up *Now*.

Paul: *Now* is all I know
now is all I got
and I don't *know*...

Charizze: *Know*ing you're fuel to my flame?
Don't look back
Don't need your *regrets*

And the game continues as long as the next in the circle of friends can provide a song that ends in the last word of a game. Pinoy Henyo on the other hand is a timed game also called Charade in English. UP CBo, the organization loves these two games that we usually skip classes already because of playing this game. We can't get back these games when we are old already and have our marriage certificate and babies. Priorities will be very different. So laugh often. Forgive often.

It was Eingels' last semester. Everytime he was asked what his course was, he would say- Various Wisdom and Knowledge or in Tagalog, Samu't Saring Kaalaman. He can play different musical instruments, he can speak different languages, and he is good in theology and philosophy and in world geography considering he travelled the world already. He has a bad penmanship but oh so well in manuscript writing. He always sleeps at his class but his grades are synonymous to excellent. I am madly in love with him simply because it's as if there's no more guy that's going to love me after him. So I am waiting for him until there's a sign that it's okay to love a new guy for me. He now has a wife and a child. I travelled abroad and the whole Philippines- from Northern Luzon to the Southernmost Philippines just to find someone who will be "The One" for me- someone new who will be my husband. But I keep on going back to my refuge, the church to give me the signs to Let Go, or Let God?

II

Space Time Travel Protected me
My future self visited me.

I have a roommate, who looks exactly like me but who is white. I am brown in color. Her name is Krystle Mei. Krystle Mei looks Chinese and I look like a Filipino. Krystle Mei is her code name just so people won't get bothered with her presence. We both have chinky eyes, same height, and same straight black long hair. Krystle Mei, Krystle Me, Krazy Me, Crazy Me. Gets? My future self guided me along the best pathway during my college years. I look like a Chinese girl in my future self. She travelled from 2017 to 2007 just to guide me during my college years. Space Time Machine is for Billionaires and for heads of the banks only. During 2017, I found out that I was a trader. Bankers use Space Time Machine to predict the dollar exchange rate around the world. That is, for greater profit for the bank.

During 2007, Krystle Mei became my roommate in Ilang-Ilang Residence Hall inside University of the Philippines, Diliman. She never really existed in my life every 9-6pm. She would only exist after school and during sleeping times. She said she's also a tourism major, but I seldom and almost not see her around our college. I admire her so much because she's a muse of a Fraternity, her family own businesses and a resort and farmlands. She's the most perfect girl in the crowd. She always teaches me to act like a princess to meet my prince. We always jog together in the acad oval and tell stories and our day to day problems. I've learned how to have bigger boobs and smaller arms just by exercising. She teaches me the hacks of modeling. She also invited us backstage of a rock star band's concert.

Her mom and dad are very good looking. Her mom in the picture is fair, and has long silky and black hair, and curvaceous. So what I did was I told my mom to have longer hair and to jog everyday to attain a beautiful body just like in her future self. My mom during that time has very short hair, and a bit chubby. Her dad is very good at holding a gun but he is in the intelligence department of the army. Little did I know that my dad is also a former army in the southern part of the Philippines?

My future self who resides in Ilang-Ilang Residence Hall in University of the Philippines Diliman perfume is Chanel. She then gave me, Victoria's Secret Pure Seduction cologne because I am with the Victorinos. Victoria's secret to know the Victorino's Secret on how to seduce that person I truly admire. She also gave me a Victoria's Secret Bag to be used whenever I'm with Eingel. She also lends me books by Robert Greene which are the Law of Power and Law of Seduction. She is showing me her pictures of her graduation and her picture with a medal. She teaches me that come what may, I would just trust in God's perfect timing because there's no really such thing as perfect. The Victorino family is very famous around the world. In UP Diliman, they have bodyguards. They have lots of second hand cars and they ride in a convoy. UP Diliman is just a public university so the Victorinos only use second hand cars so that thieves won't snatch their belongings.

Winner takes it all; the Victorinos have all the things they wanted. They are all chubby and tall people implicitly telling everyone that they have feast always in their kitchen and tables. Winner takes it all, that's what my future self, Krystle Mei wanted me to understand. No matter how difficult the journey seems to be, just have faith with that person for Mr. Engiel Airano Victorino. I can cry all I want, but when I fall asleep, things will be alright soon. She became my guide in whatever purpose God has given me. 2017, we will see each other again after this semester. She told me that I am a forex trader. One decade, I don't know how life would change. But without her, life would be full of destruction and there will be no more hope. Life is unbearable.

Winner takes it all. Krystle Mei, teaches me to be contented and happy along the way. There are no perfect conditions so might as well be happy. Whatever situation I am in, God is in control so always being thankful in every way. Life is about taking risks. Whether life gives you so much failure and you're on the losing end, God will give you light to walk upon as guidance. Krystle Mei always gave me her food whenever I feel down and depressed and she would only eat outside or order food at a fast food. She's really nice and her alto voice is very seductive to guys. She is the muse of a fraternity in UP when we were together. Whenever we jog around academic oval, she said that working in the bank is the only job that she knew that is very lucrative and has a very good standing in organizational chart. In human being's timeline, there will be no contentment. When you're in high school all we ever wanted was to pass UP College Admission Test. When I had a pending case result, I entered UP Baguio. I studied so hard to pass UP Diliman. I have sleepless nights just to focus on my academics. Now, I am a choir member in the grand temple, a BS Tourism student who resides with my future self, who teaches me how to be the best person that I can be.

Space Time Travel is the best gift, the universe has offered me during that semester. Krystle Mei, my pseudo name gave me a wide range of perspectives because of her space time travel. Indeed Crazy Me or Krystle Mei are just word play but it helped me recuperate from all the anxieties- the loneliness of being alone and being a kid in the wide universe of UP Diliman.

III

Hope versus hope, vow versus vow

I really don't know why every time I have to be in other's arms to be loved, I 'm getting sick, or the other guy is getting sick. My officemate in currency trading, Migz Aboitiz, keeps on telling me that he loves me, and then he got pneumonia.He is the unico hijo of the Aboitiz Shipping Company. He is my best friend who loves to be my so called body guard and laugh tremendously.

My British boss in a five star hotel, Sir Neil O'Connor says "I love you Leslie" every time were together in his office, but eventually I got dengue and got hospitalized for two weeks. Good thing it's not Japanese encephalitis or else I'm dead! I loved Engiel so much that it tears me apart. I know I have to let go, but letting go means Letting God. Letting God orchestrate if he is for me, Eingel will come back to me. 5 years has passed, and he is still not here, I don't know when he is coming back, but I know he will.

Today, me and Eingel Airano are together again at Villiam Luna City. Inside Villiam Luna City, there's a prestigious school, a very majestic church and a Villiam Luna BJMP where we go together. I learned to let go of all the people who tells me that they have a crush on me, simply because I made a promise when I was in college, that I will love Eingel Airano and get married to him. But it never happened. He got married to Jashmine Naumay. It was really embarrassing. Why am I saying my prayers that I will love my close friend and get married to him when I finish my academics? We stayed together in Villiam Luna City for about three years. He has a kid now, a wife, a business. He is the CEO of a TV Channel. I really don't know why I said that to my prayers. I don't want to be with them anymore. But it keeps on hunting me. It is hope versus hope. I just want to live here and now. Eingel Airano Victorino is living in Quezon City and my family is in Sultan Kudarat-A province very far from the metro. I made a vow to the God that I serve, as a ticket to pass my thesis. A heart ache from a billionaire, that's what I am getting. I loved him so much that every single day, I am thinking that probably, when he looks his face in the mirror, he would remember me. Because I keep on mirroring him, how he laughs, how he loves his white top and black pants, how he smiles, and how he loves to hold his IPAD, how he cheers his favorite football team, how he sways his butt every time he feels happy. I became a model and even got featured in Billboard in EDSA. I hope he got into traffic when my billboard was aired. I hope he remembers me. I hope he remembers how we laugh, how we cry, how we dine together, how we watched together his favorite football game. He is six foot one guy who always love to be with his IPAD, and gaming console.

When he eats, he eats 5 plates of rice and viand per meal and he loves chocolates. I miss him so much. I miss how he cuddles me. How I play with his man boobs and his tummy. He's very neat. But his penmanship is a bit ugly. He loves to listen to music. His favorite radio station is 95.5FM. He loves rock music. I remember he was crying in front of me because I call him, "Fat, fat, fat". His eyes were very teary, it really breaks my heart. I said sorry but I can't stop his crying. I don't know why he looks like that right now. He is fat but not healthy, fat. He is pinkish and fat again like the cartoon character Maginboo in Dragon Ball Z? Is his penmanship the same or better? We laugh, cry, eat, quarrel and at the end of the day we leave V. Luna and just forget each other.

When I was riding in MRT, going to Makati from Quezon Avenue, I vowed that I will never go back to Quezon City again- to the place where I meet him. But all of a sudden, the train where I am located had a smoke and it feels like I'm gonna be suffocated, seriously? S.E.R.I.O.U.S.L.Y? God is looking for my promise? He is now a married man. It is the entire company that I'm gonna be leading with Eingel when I will marry him. I talk to a high ranking official of a church, the minister said, that yes it will come true. Just wait and see God's mighty hand and how he will make things all work together for good. I can marry the guy that I prayed for because of all the signs.

Every single day, before going to work, I kneel and pray for guidance. I work as a currency trader. I took a Certificate in Financial Markets Professional with Bloomberg in New Era University. Then I have a Practicum in Singapore Financial District. For two weeks, I travelled and roamed around Singapore. Eat the finest food and experienced the luxury lifestyle of Marina Bay Sands. Having the financial markets certification from Bloomberg is the reason why I can trade currencies. We have meetings with the big boss of Metro bank Singapore, Philippine National Bank Singapore and Banco De Oro or BDO Singapore and the daughter of the Head of Central Bank of the Philippines during that time. It was so surreal. I also met the owner of RCBC. She's Chinese but her eyes are not that chinky. Would you imagine? A woman is in front of me, talking to me and she's already the daughter of the UN Ambassador and owner of a bank? I don't know what I did in the past, but being with this people made me feel so blessed. Staying in Bloomberg Philippines and Bloomberg Singapore is not a normal thing for me. What I can't forget about Bloomberg is that they can teach people how to predict things. Predict how the market runs, whether it is going to be a bull market or a bear market. And of course, profit from that prediction. I remember my former professor who is the President and Chief Executive Officer of Philippine Airlines and SEAIR which became Tiger Airways, he would always say to us to always read news because it teaches people how to predict what's going to happen next. Owners of Philippine Airlines and Bloomberg are billionaires and their territory is around the world. Being in University of the Philippines Asian Institute of Tourism can teach you the glitz and glamour of the world to get to places and get the things that we want, but taking the Certification with Bloomberg is no longer superficial. It's money!!! It's moolah baby!!! Trading currencies, I learned that I can earn $1000 in just one day-even if I'm just at home, and in the Philippines. I am earning dollars in the Philippines. I have higher income than my cousin who works in Middle East as a nurse. I love tourism and foreign exchange trading so much that money comes to me easily and frequently. Tourism is a study of discretionary income and discretionary time.

Meeting that Manager for PNB Asia and the Pacific, who is based in Singapore, taught me lots of things. She writes books… academic books. I wanted to be like her but in different way. I know I am not that good in Math, and Ms. Cristy is a Math major or in University of the Philippines Los Banos. She's very smart and pretty as well. She was wearing black dress during the meeting. She's a typical UPian, and knowing her makes me so thankful about my parents who gave me the chance to study in UP Diliman. My parents always instill in me the saying, "If you think education is expensive, take ignorance". "Education is the only thing that you can inherit from us, so you have to study so well." Being with bankers and telling us how to become like them makes my dream bridging the gap from dreams to reality a little smaller. It's like telling us and guiding us to trust the process.

We may be small at first, but eventually, we'll reap the successes in due time.

The owner of the bank of RCBC, inspired me the most. She's Mam Margaret. Her words are like music to my ears. Especially when she said that, "Your like my mom, her first job is in forex trading." The words are like lullaby. What is she implying? Am I gonna own a bank someday? I have a distorted reality. Being with billionaires is a bit making me crazy. I don't want to make lame excuses. But if she believes that I'm like her mom, probably I can own a bank someday. Probably, now it seems crazy. But someday, with some twist of faith, probably, it would happen. Being with Ms. Margaret, listening to her words of wisdom and advice on career and bank transactions in is the best gift my Singapore trip ever gave me. It's an experience that I won't exchange for anything.

I also met the daughter of the Head of Central Bank of the Philippines. She's managing Nu Skin Singapore. She's not like Mam Margaret. Mam Margaret, if very unforgettable because her words resonates success, not only for her kin's legacy but her words also echoes to my whole being- making me a renewed human being because of the hope that I can be like them someday.

I cannot imagine that this influential people are just talking to me, walking around my social circle and telling me stories about their ups and downs and how they become successful. It's like seating around to different people and asking them, "How to be you po?" Every single day of my Singapore trip, in Singapore Financial District is very exciting that leads me to become the best version of myself. My roommate. Ms. Go was my idol when I was a kid. She is a Chinese lady, who is a muse of a fraternity in UP Diliman. She graduated Comlaude in her degree. She's like me who took up BS Social Sciences in UP Baguio when we were in first year. But she's just one year ahead from me.

IV

Pick your Role Model Wisely, Find out what they did, and do it.

Ever since I was a kid, my mom is my role model. She is very pretty and very smart. I love her so much that I win Math quiz bees in the hope that I can be like her, an owner of a ready to wear shop. She's a chemical engineer by profession and speaks different languages. Yes, I am acing my exams and quizzes in Chemistry when I was in high school. Simply because my mom is my confidante, my idol, and simply because, I'm a chemical engineer wanna be too who sells clothes because there is more money in selling clothes that just by being an employee as an engineer. My mom always tell me, if I am an employee, I have money every 15th and 30th. If I am a business person, I have money, every single day.

My dad is my idol too because she has lots of farmland and sells sidecar as a business. He taught me how to work hard for myself, because life is hard. People only love themselves and people will love you when they need you. So always love your family because they will back you up no matter what. That is what is instilled in me because of my dad's words of wisdom.

Chef Sau del Rosario was also my idol. I worked in F1 Hotel in Taguig. He is a very influential man at his 40's. He travelled the world. He studied culinary in Paris, France. He taught me the secrets in cooking in a five star hotel. He is just like my girl roommate in UP- Krus na Ligas, probably because he also took his undergraduate program in UP Diliman. His degree is BS Hotel Restaurant and Institution Management. He is also a Kapampangan. Pampanga is best known as the culinary capital of the Philippines. He is indeed a pride of our country. I can't study culinary in Europe anymore. Seating in front of him while we were eating lunch and talking about our experiences in UP makes me no longer want to go Europe to study culinary. Taking lessons from him is a great experience.

A Sumacomlaude of Yale of Religion and Music is someone I look up too, together with his wife, Sir Tony and Ms. Gem. His wife is a music major in UP Diliman and took up accountancy in New Era University. What I did was, I took BS Tourism, became a choir member in Templo Central and take up financial markets lessons with Bloomberg. Being a choir member in Templo Central is like being a voice major in UP- College of Music. I took up Financial markets because it's somehow will suffice my financial literacy which is needed in the world where I can travel to different place if ever God gave me again the opportunity to travel. Ms. Gem is a Music Major in UP and Accountancy major in New Era University, while I am a Tourism Major in UP and Financial Markets Professional New Era University.

Alma Concepcion is a beauty queen, actress, model, UP Diliman graduate, and businesswoman. She's my seatmate in my subject Anthropolgy 10. Her brother, Albert is a flight attendant of Philippine Airlines. She taught me how to be as pretty as her. How to walk, how to talk, how to eat, how to drink. Basically, simple gestures to to a wanna-be beauty queen. She was a former drug addict. But what I've learned from her is that she has everything life has to offer. Money, wealth, youthful beauty, intellect, and fame- what can a girl could wish for? She became arrogant, no the word is not arrogant. It's hubris! By then, I learned to humble myself before her. Winner takes it all can sometimes a bit scary. It goes in to your head. And boomerang! It shatters your whole being! Being in the airport and being accused as a shabu addict is very shameful, considering there are many cameras watching your actions because you're very famous.

My sister has always been my inspiration to be the best that I can be. She became the President of our organization inside UP Diliman campus and is now the President of Development Bank of Singapore. She is now living in Singapore but she contacts our whole family every single day. Meeting different big players of bankers inside the country and Asia keeps the gap small between the two of us. She is a perfectionist unlike me. She has an excellent leadership skills and very intellectual in solving math problems. She is a statistician and took up a certification also in National University of Singapore- the top university in Asia.

Short Story by
Charles Tomeldan

Love Underground

January 30, 1945. World War II had been raging for years.

In the city of Manila, the district of Ermita rocked as cannons pounded the area.

The whole of the Philippines had been under Japanese rule for more than three years, and American forces were closing in on Manila, bent on liberating the once-free city.

Christian dodged the shelling as he crossed Taft Avenue, searching for a house where he could take refuge.

The bombings had become more often, and Japanese troops scoured the city looking for supplies that they could seize.

Christian was living in an underground flat, right below his friend's apartment, when Japanese troops swooped down on his neighborhood that morning and scanned the row of apartments where his buddy's unit stood on one end. His friend had left the unit when the city was invaded. Fearful that his cubbyhole would be discovered by the Japs, Christian left in a hurry, tucking a .38-caliber revolver on his lower back.

A shell exploded a few meters from Christian, and he scurried in the opposite direction. He turned into an alley and found a run-down building and barged through the door that was boarded up.

******

Julienne sat in a corner of the cellar and covered her ears as the explosions continued. The blasts were so loud that she could hear them even when she lived underground, and she was startled as a bomb exploded nearby.

The past days were an ordeal for her. She lived alone in the basement, surviving on the meager provisions that she found in a cupboard. The food had dwindled, and her doubts soon turned into anxiety.

She heard footsteps on the floor above the cellar. The footsteps came to a halt right above the trap door that led to her hideout. Julienne shivered in fear.

The trap door opened with a creak, and her instincts forced her to grab a baseball bat that lay by her side. The wooden bat was the only weapon that she could find in the cellar, and she had always placed it where she could reach it if the need arises. A weapon to use to defend herself from an unseen enemy.

Muscular legs descended the rickety stairs and an athletic-looking man landed on the cement floor.

Julienne rose to her feet and screamed, tightly gripping the bat, "Don't hurt me!"

Christian raised his hands slowly. "I won't hurt you, miss."

"Who are you?" Julienne demanded, her heart-shaped face showing fright.

"I'm Christian. It's okay, you don't need the bat, I'm not with the Japs."

Julienne relaxed and lowered the bat. "I'm Julienne. What brought you here?"

"The bombings had become more frequent by the day and the Japs had raided the place where I live. I was holed up in a cellar similar to this and left as soon as I saw the Japs making their way to the unit. Ran across the avenue and turned into your alley. I entered the building and I found the trap door. Does that answer your question?"

"It sure does," Julienne retorted.

"How long have you been staying in this hole?" It was Christian's turn to ask.

"Three days and two nights."

"How did you end up here?" Christian probed.

Julienne narrated the events that occurred a few days back. She was working in a tertiary hospital as an orderly. Last Saturday, a new company of Japanese soldiers filled in for their comrades that had been guarding the hospital for months. The new commanding-in-chief, a major, took a liking to her. The chief nurse, a Filipina, noticed and anticipated what could happen. She and Julienne planned her escape. The next day, she left under cover of darkness. She wandered around the city and found the deserted building. She slipped through and found the cellar.

"What about food?" Christian asked, his stomach grumbling.

"There's nothing much left." Julienne pointed toward the cupboard.

Christian made his way to the cupboard and opened it. He grimaced at the sight of the sparse canned food. "This will only last for a couple of days."

"What are we going to do?"

"I'll go to the market first thing in the morning and see what I can find. But for now, I'll get some rest. Running from the Japs was exhausting." Christian spotted the bed with crumpled sheets. The sheets looked as if they had not been washed for months."

"Sorry, I never got around to washing them. Water's scarce here", Julienne apologized.

"Don't be. You should save water before it runs out." Christian jumped onto the bed. He dozed off and was soon asleep."

***

Christian awoke at the crack of dawn. He gazed at Julienne, who was sleeping on the concrete floor. He shook her gently, and she was roused from a shallow sleep.

"I'll go to the market now. Will you be all right?" Julienne nodded.

Christian glanced at his revolver lying on the side table. He hesitated for a moment. "Here, take my gun, in case someone else comes down to the basement. Do you know how to use this?"

Julienne shook her head, so Christian showed her how.

***

The sky was overcast on that day. The market was abuzz with activity when Christian arrived. The sky was overcast, so he did not waste time and went briskly around the market, searching for essentials that the few centavos in his pocket could buy. Food was hard to come by since the invasion, and Christian haggled and bargained with vendors and in one store, had to trade his watch to buy six kilos of rice, a live chicken, and a few cans of meat.

Mateo, Christian's childhood pal, saw him as he paid the vendor. Mateo approached and nudged Christian. The latter was visibly surprised to see Mateo.

"Have you heard of the rumor?" Mateo asked.

"No. Fill me in."

"The Americans are coming. To free the city from the Japs. Be prepared."

Mateo walked away before Christian could say another word. He saw why.

A platoon of Japanese soldiers trudged through the market, stopping every so often to check the marketgoers' identification papers. Fear gripped Christian, for he had lost his papers in one of the firefights he participated in when Manila was invaded.

A *kariton*[1] made of wood and rubber was left under a *sampaloc*[2] tree and Christian immediately run toward it. He climbed into the cart and hid under the hay.

The soldiers were getting closer to where Christian hid. They stopped when they reached the **sampaloc** tree and stood to one side of the *kariton* and smoked. They chatted in *Nihongo*[3] as Christian lay motionless in the cart.

Christian held his breath; he dared not move. His heart was racing. The moment seemed to pass slowly for Christian. It felt like an eternity.

The soldiers, done with their short break, moved on to inspect the marketgoers. Their voices faded away and soon Christian was left all by himself.

He took a peek, making sure the soldiers are gone. He climbed out of the kariton and looked in the direction of the troops. The soldiers were a quarter of a mile away.

---

[1] *a pushcart*
[2] *tamarind*
[3] *Japanese language*

Thunder rumbled overhead and rain fell at once in buckets, and Christian hurried back to Julienne.

***

Julienne heard footsteps above and the trap door opened. The stairs creaked as the footsteps approached. She raised the revolver and pointed it toward the intruder.

Christian came into view, his entire body wet from the rain. He raised his arms in defense. "Hey, it's me." Julienne sighed and lowered the gun.

"Did everything go well?"

Christian recounted the close encounter he had with the Japanese soldiers.

Julienne was relieved. "That was a close call."

"You bet it was. Let's have lunch. You're cooking." Christian winked at Julienne.

"Not until you dry yourself first," she berated.

Christian took off his polo, pants, and slip-ons, then he grabbed a bath towel hanging by a rack and began to dry himself." Julienne helped him dry his back. She gently wiped the back of his torso, down to his waist. He turned and kissed her on the lips. She did not resist.

***

She cooked rice and *tinolang manok*[4]. She was a good cook, and Christian nodded in approval. He gobbled all the food and left not a morsel on his plate.

"How did you learn to cook so well?"

"My mom taught me."

"She must be a great cook."

"She was." Her mother died during the early bombings of the city. She was consumed by grief at once and it showed. Christian knew better, and he never asked about Julienne's mother as they ate.

They lay in bed as evening fell.

Julienne popped a question, "I don't know you that much, except that you carry a gun. Tell me about yourself."

Christian recounted that he was a national shooting champion and that he taught the sport in an indoor shooting range before war broke out and the Japanese seized the city, and in an instant, everything changed. He left before the Japs stormed the range and took over.

"I don't know much about you either, except that you hold a bat," Christian said in jest. Julienne giggled unabashedly. She began to tell her story.

She was born in a laid-back town in Nueva Vizcaya. Her father died when she was in her teens, and her mother was forced to leave town and bring her to

---

[4] *chicken broth*

Manila where opportunities were plentiful. She took a course in midwifery and earned a living working as an orderly in a hospital a few blocks away. Then the war changed her life.

She turned to glance at Christian, but he was deep in slumber.

***

Julienne was the first to rise from the bed. She cooked a heavy breakfast that consisted of scrambled eggs, baked beans, and *sinangag*[5].

"Breakfast is ready, sleepyhead," she teased Christian, but he lay still in bed. She came near and sat beside him.

"Are you okay?" she asked. Christian didn't reply. She lay her hand on his forehead. It was hot to the touch. "You're running a fever," she said, a look of concern on her face. She went to the medicine cabinet and opened it. The cabinet was bare.

Julienne closed her eyes and breathed long. She had to make a decision. She put on an orange wool jacket and knotted a scarf around her neck and turned to Christian. "I'm going out. I'll look for medicine so we can reduce your fever. Christian raised his hand heavily in protest, but she was up the stairs and out of the building.

***

---

[5] *fried rice*

Julienne looked sideways, making sure that no troops were approaching. There were none, not by a mile. Julienne walked for three blocks and came to a hospital that bore the ravages of war. The hospital was where she used to work before the Japanese major and his troops came and took control of the institution and she ran away.

She cautiously made her way to the back where a low green gate was carved on the concrete wall, hidden by the bushes. She brushed aside the undergrowth and went past the gate, crouching as she did.

A gray-haired nurse on the first floor happened to look down a window and saw Julienne as she gingerly crossed the backyard. She whistled curtly so that no one would hear except Julienne, and the orderly glanced up. Julienne waved at her frantically and the elderly nurse waved back.

Julienne touched her neck with the back of her hand as if to mimic fever. The nurse understood. She disappeared and returned to the window a minute later. In her hand was a bottle filled with red syrup that was formulated to relieve fever, and she tossed it at Julienne.

The female orderly deftly caught the bottle of medicine with two hands. She blew a kiss to the nurse, and the nurse waved goodbye.

Julienne left in haste, passing through the secret gate.

***

Christian was sound asleep when she arrived. She approached and shook his shoulder gently, and he stirred. He rubbed his eyes and she opened the bottle and gave him a tablespoon of the syrup. He shrank back in bed get to get more shut-eye.

She fixed him a bowl of soup in the afternoon and gave him another tablespoon of the medicine.

Night descended on the city. They had a light dinner and Christian took another spoonful of the medicine.

***

Christian's fever broke the following morning. He sat upright on the bed and stretched and told Julienne, "My ammunition's running low, I'm going back to the shooting range to get some." But Julienne would not let him. "You just came from sick bay."

"Every hour counts in this war."

He put on outdoor clothes that he found in a closet and walked back toward the bed where Julienne sat on the edge. He kissed her on the forehead.

Christian mounted stairs and was gone.

***

The avenue was devoid of troops, and Christian took the chance and walked briskly for more than a mile until he reached Quezon Boulevard. He entered a side street and the shooting range emerged.

The dilapidated building had borne the brunt of war. Holes caused by mortar shells dotted the facade, and windows were either smashed or boarded up. Christian surveyed the building for noise inside. There was none, and he broke in through an opening on a window.

He burst into his office and was dismayed to find that it was in a pitiful state. He pushed the large glass-topped table and knelt on the floor. His hands felt for the loose panel. It was under the board where he hid a tin box full of bullets when he first learned of the news about the Japanese troops' arrival. His right hand found the removable panel and he lifted the tile.

The tin box containing the bullets was gone.

"Hold it right there!" A female voice.

Steadily, Christian stood, his back against the woman.

"Don't do something stupid," the woman warned. Christian heard the sound of a rifle being cocked.

He raised his arms and said, "I'm unarmed!"

"Turn around!"

Christian did as he was told, and he was greeted by the nozzle of a rifle. It was pointed at his nose.

***

The woman lowered the rifle. "Is that you, Christian?" she asked, bewildered."

"Rachel?"

"In the flesh." And she gave him a tight hug.

Rachel and Christian were instructors in the shooting range before the war erupted in the city. She loved him and did not hide it. Her affection for him was one-way, though. He had no feelings for her.

Now, seeing Christian again, the flames of Rachel's love for him were rekindled.

"I can't breathe, Rachel."

"Sorry." Rachel released Christian from her embrace. "Why did you come back here?"

"Ammo," Christian said, pointing his index finger at the false panel.

"Sorry to disappoint you, but you won't find anything." She turned to her companions. There were five, each with a rifle slung on his shoulder. "We came here at daybreak and searched the place. We could not find any ammo."

Christian's shoulders slumped.

"But there's a ton of guns and ammo in a place we're raiding," Rachel tried to douse Christian's disappointment. Suddenly, his eyes brightened. He was a sucker for action, and he took every chance that he could get for some.

"When?" Christian quizzed.

"Tomorrow, before dawn, when it's darkest."

"Where?"

"An armory guarded by Japs. A couple of miles from here."

"Count me in."

"I knew you'd say that. Be back here at three in the morning."

Christian rushed back home.

***

Back in the basement, Christian told Julienne of the chance meeting he had with Rachel, and the raid they were staging in the wee hours of the morning.

Julienne was extremely worried. "I have a bad feeling about this, Christian."

The action buff just ignored her.

"I can't let you go this time. You're precious to me."

"You're a treasure, Rachel, but I have to do this. I don't wish to stay here when the Americans return because I have a gun without bullets."

Julienne could do nothing to talk Christian out of it.

***

They had dinner and went straight to bed. Their backs were turned against each other; both would not say a word and kept mum throughout the evening. The silence that hung was deafening. Midnight came and they fell asleep

The couple awoke to the sound of heavy and frequent shelling.

In the city's outskirts, American tanks and troops armed to the teeth started their advance, anticipating the confrontation with the Japanese that lay ahead.

The Japanese troops in the city stood their ground, ready to engage the Yanks in a wide-scale firefight.

The Battle of Manila would soon begin.

Christian dressed up and grabbed the revolver. Julienne tried to stop him from leaving.

"It sounds like it's hell out there. Please don't leave, Christian." He would not hear of any of it. He had thought about the raid over last night, and nothing could change his mind.

"I'll be back. You can count on it." Christian turned and left the basement, leaving Julienne helpless.

Christian climbed the stairs two steps at a time and was gone. Tears welled in Julienne's eyes.

***

Rachel and her band were waiting at the door when Christian arrived.

"Are you ready?"

"You bet," said Christian unequivocally.

Rachel handed him a rifle. "Here, you might need this." Christian examined the rifle and nodded. "Let's go."

***

The raid was partially successful. The band was able to seize rifles and boxes of ammo, but three of the men fell, leaving only Christian, Rachel, and two of the raiders to haul their loot.

They stormed out of the armory, with Rachel in the lead and Christian close behind. Up ahead, atop a roof of a five-story building, a Japanese sniper peaked inconspicuously and aimed his rifle at Rachel.

He fired, and the bullet hit Rachel's neck, and she slumped on the ground. The sniper took another aim, this time at Christian, but the shooting champion was already squeezing the trigger of his rifle. The bullet hit the sniper between the eyes and he disappeared from sight.

Christian fell to his knees and cuddled Rachel. Blood was spurting from her neck. "I feel cold, Christian." He wrapped her in his strong arms. Tears were streaming from his eyes. A moment later Rachel's slender body turned limp.

Felipe, one of the last remaining raiders, said, "There's nothing we can do, Christian." He lifted Rachel's body and trotted away.

Christian got hold of himself and ran back to the woman who had captured his heart.

***

"Julienne! Julienne!" Christian yelled as he raced down the stairs. He landed on the cellar floor and called Julienne's name again, but there was no sign of her.

Her dresses were strewn on the bed and her suitcase was open. Christian was suddenly racked with terror. "Oh, no! The Japs might have taken her," he thought dreadfully.

He turned and abruptly left the cellar.

Christian charged through the doorway as a U.S. Army jeep approached. He flagged the jeep and it came to a halt.

The sergeant on the passenger seat said, "Hop in, cowboy. We're going back to the evacuation camp." Without a word, Christian heaved himself into the back. He sat in silence and wept.

The jeep wound through the streets of Manila as bombs fell on the city.

***

The stairs grated as soldiers came down the cellar. By instinct, Julienne opened the drawer to get the revolver. She stiffened. The drawer was empty. She remembered that Christian took the gun when he left.

She braced for what would happen next.

***

The soldiers appeared and Julienne was relieved. They were Americans. The man in the lead took a couple of steps forward. His combat uniform had the insignia of a captain. He spoke, "I'm Captain Thomas." His voice had an air of authority.

"I'm glad to see you, captain."

"We gotta leave. I've got orders to take in every living civilian that we could find."

Julienne grabbed a suitcase and began to pack her clothes."

"Sorry, ma'am, but we have no time for that. We have to go."

Julienne started to object, but a corporal grabbed her arm and led her up the stairs.

She turned and took a sweeping look at the basement. This was the nest where she and Christian spent what could be the most memorable days and nights of their lives. She mused that she would not see Christian again. Instantly, a deep sense of sadness swept over her.

***

Half an hour later, the army jeep reached the encampment and Christian got off. He walked aimlessly around the camp until he came to a long tent. A red cross was emblazoned on top of the opening.

He parted the canvas and entered the tent silently. A migraine attack had crept in, and he needed to pop a pill to dull the pain. He looked around the tent. All the medics were attending to the injured that lay in beds that lined both sides of the tent.

Someone called out his name, "Christian!" He whirled and his heart jumped with joy.

Standing several meters away, a roll of bandage in her hand, was Julienne.

She ran toward him and both stood inches apart. The couple locked in a loving embrace, oblivious of the patients who watched in awe.

He said, "I thought I lost you."

"Not in this lifetime," she replied.

Outside the camp, the battle raged on, but Christian and Julienne did not hear a sound.

Short Story by Satabdi Saha

The Mansion

Nilima stared outside the window, fascinated by the storm that raced through the garden and lashed the trees with a vitriolic force of a monster on the rampage. Windows rattled, calendars flew off the walls, papers floated, utensils fell cluttering the floor, but she was unmoved. The spray spurted inside, wetting her bed, her pillow, her body. Slowly, as the rage subsided, Nilima fell into a languor, the wetness somehow calming the turbulence inside her. She fell asleep on the moist armchair and dreamt again the same dream.

The huge mansion looked serenely beautiful, glinting in the last rays of the setting sun. Glossy pillars, black marbled steps, mosaic floors, carpeted halls, plush curtains, dazzling chandeliers----and Nili, as everyone called her, on her mother's knee in the garden. Then, the inevitable----the rusting, peeling, breaking, dissolving into rubble, after which a phenomenal upthrust—an ugly blackened face ; diabolical—rising out of the netherworld, rising up, reaching for her. Startled, Nili woke up. She couldn't fathom the reason behind this repetitive dream. Her heart - wrenching cries reverberated inside the still, decrepit, almost a wreck of a house. They magnified, ran amok, hurtling through the dusty gloom of corridors, past the stairs to the garden. The rain had stopped. The afternoon drifted to purple and shadows of trees began to lengthen, describing sinister patterns on walls where darkness connived with yawning cavities of brick and sand.

Nili went to the terrace. She knew that the nightmares were nothing but the fall-out of her angst, eating into her existence. But somehow the explanation was not satisfactory. She leant over the parapet and looked down. Below, there was darkness and only darkness. The nearby houses were lit up and the mingled sounds of bells and conch shells of evening pujas began. Nili sighed. She couldn't forget that face of her dreams. The devilish puckering of lips seemed so attractive ! She was shocked. Her once inchoate longing for a mate grew stronger with age. Nili touched the coarse boundary that circumscribed her own life, with passionate intensity. She was fifty. Her tortuous journey through the torrid zones alone, in the flush of her youth was perhaps a nemesis for an unrecognised sin, she thought.

Nili was not pretty. Not even pleasant to look at. She was born in Dhaka before the partition of India in 1947. After independence, her father, a merchant, moved to Purulia in West Bengal. There he built a two-storied house and lived resplendently with his only child, wife and a retinue of servants. Nili lacked nothing. She went to a local school, passed the matric examination and stayed at home with her parents, in wait for a prospective groom. Neighbouring families were too poor for the Sen family to associate with. Rich youths with impressive backgrounds did not take a second look at her. And so Nili, companionless, aged. Surprisingly, in spite of her wealth, none made advances to her. After her father's death, she was left alone, trussed with the house. Yet Nili did not go to work, even though the expenses of maintaining the house did not become any cheaper. She thrived on her father's bank balance, but that too shrivelled with time. Getting rid of the servants, she fell to doing the household chores alone which of course helped to devour some bland hours of her life. Neighbours were few and friends or relatives fewer and far between. Standing on the terrace Nili wept, as the permeating smell of rain in the late evening air filled her nostrils.

One day, Vinay Sen, her father, came home carrying a packet. Eagerly unwrapping it, ten-year old Nili screamed with terror. He laughed, while her mother was visibly angry and shocked. Inside the wrapper was a hideous mask. The eyes somehow looked different, even though frightfully menacing. They seemed to attract, mesmerise. Nili's father, so unlike his character, bought it as if under a spell, to amuse his little girl (who was getting pretty bored with the usual insipid fare of toys) from a roadside shop, whose owner was ready to sell it at half the price. The mask was made of paper- mache; one of the many found in Purulia for which it is famous. Apart from the roguish eyes, the face, sinuous with pockets of untidy beard, looked as if the dirt of centuries' mischief lurked there. Nili's mother, aghast at the sight, shouted in disgust at her husband.

'Couldn't you find something better than this ghoulish face to gift your daughter?'

'Why, it's so different from your other masks ! Isn't it my pet? I guess, you are not silly to be frightened because it's ugly!'

'Why, what nonsense! Silly! She is only ten!'

With trembling hands Nili lifted the mask. She had to prove that she wasn't frightened. Not frightened at all!

From then on grew Nili's uncanny affinity with the demonic visage. She carried it along with her through the huge mansion, talking, whispering, playing with it. Contrary to her nature, Nili wore the mask as if egged on by someone, to terrorize her mother, who hated the sight of it.

'Do you have to wear that horrid thing, do you?' she asked, shuddering.

'Mummy, he's my friend. He talks to me you know ; he's not bad, not bad at all. I like him.' Her mother's face whitened with the premonition of Nili's bizarre leanings. She severely reprimanded her daughter.

'Throw it out immediately Nili ! I won't have you wearing and talking nonsense with it. Throw it out at once!'

'But ma, he hasn't hurt me. I don't have any friends except Dipa. But she doesn't play with me everyday and hates him. But he stays with me all the time and speaks and plays with me. I love him mummy', replied the distressed child, pointing at the mask.

Anima trembled with inexplicable fear. She cursed her husband. Seizing the mask from Nili's hand, she threw it outside on the rubbish bin and for the first time gave her child a resounding slap on the cheek.

'That will put you in place. Toying with the devil! What a father----!' She gnashed her teeth and left the room. Nili cried, tears flooding her face. At night she dreamt of the mask and the rubbish can. The eyes beckoned her. The bewitching eyes! She woke up in the wee hours of the morning and unnoticed went outside. The thing was still there. Throwing away all her inhibitions, she gingerly picked up the mask with her left hand and went to the courtyard. No one was around. On a nearby tree, crows made eerie noises. Nili opened the tap and let the water run on it. Then slowly, with the frill of her dress, she wiped it clean and went inside. Her room was still dark. A faint streak of morning light filtered through the slits between the curtains. The eyes were looking at her. With a little shiver she kissed the lips, climbed a chair and tossed the mask on top of a remote, dust-laden corner of a cupboard, not observable by anyone. But in her hurry to hide the forbidden object in semi-darkness, Nili failed to notice that her favourite plaything fell from the targeted place and was wedged between the rear boards of the furniture and the wall, from where it disappeared into oblivion. That day suddenly Anima collapsed with high fever and in spite of the best of treatments she died within a week.

The devastating loss in Nili's life was enough to erase even the vestige of memory of the mask. As she grew old, all her concern centred on her father who was greatly altered after his wife's death. Her free hours were spent mostly roaming around the house and garden. Mr.Sen's efforts in securing a husband for his daughter did not mature. Prospective grooms scuttled away when they saw her and even the lure of the lucre failed to bring them back. Gradually she gave up being concerned about her marital prospects. But Mr. Sen was desperate to get her settled. To Nili's utter exasperation, unemployed, middle-aged men were wooed with the intention of getting a stay-in son- in-law.

'Father, what do you really want? Marry me with any baggage and drown me? Or do you want me to walk out of this house?' Her father couldn't utter a word. Relatives came in droves, trying to act as intermediaries between father and daughter. Nili drove them out of the house. She wanted to be alone. The huge mansion was intoxicating. She flitted from room to room talking to herself. It was as if the house waited for communication. Her bedroom in the southern corner of the building was her favourite. She spent long hours, minutely observing a little crack on the rear wall near the cupboard. The servants laughed, thinking that her psychic peregrinations were only for a long-lost love.

Mr. Sen died suddenly of a stroke when Nili was forty. Suddenly there was a hiatus between Nili's pragmatic self and the other one, who entertained her, accompanied her throughout the house and perambulated through her wildest fantasies. Yet certain practical considerations had to be taken into account. She had to survive and survive alone. The mansion weaved a spell around her. Getting rid of the servants, she fell to working alone; cleaning, dusting, washing. The world outside, though meaningless now to her, had to be confronted. Monthly visits to the bank, settling accounts, paying dues, weekly shopping, continued. These necessities tapered from the regular to the infrequent and finally to the rare. Neighbours saw her walking alone to the market. Whispers buzzed in the air.

'Wonder how she lives alone, in that great house!'

'She's crazy, you know, that's why. Look, there she goes talking to herself—'

'Surprising, she isn't scared living alone like this!'

'None goes near that old house after dark!'

'Her eyes, so strange, aren't they?'

Nili imbibed the scent of disapproval in the air and recoiled in disgust. How she hated those petty women! It was revolting to think that she had once entertained the idea of renting the house! She went indoors, tears welling up in her eyes, seeing the fading colours of her beautiful house, the riot of creepers in the corners and the run-on cracks on the walls, exposing its lacerated veins. It was beyond her means to restore it. The garden, once so full of flowers, wouldn't thrive no matter how much she slaved. It was full of ugly clumps of grass. The trees, most of which stood like leafless skeletons, mocked her. At night, she retired to her own little room and stared vacantly for hours at the peeling plasters and the crack that travelled aimlessly along the wall of her room. She smiled like a clairvoyant in communication with someone who responded to her from somewhere. Often she fell asleep while ruminating and dreamt the same dream.

Nili's self- imposed isolation distanced her neighbours so much that few ever came to enquire after her. The gradual transmutation of a cheerful young girl to a surly old woman who kept to herself, muttering gibberish, only raised speculations about her sanity. Deliberately, queries of concerned neighbours were made redundant by hints of interference. Offers of help were sternly rejected. She grew old, oblivious to the demands of her body. In the mirror Nili saw wrinkles; saw criss- crossing cracks on the walls of her room—her tanned skin standing out against the darkened paint that chronicled the wasted years of her youth. Looking at herself she cried. A burst of uncontrolled, heart –wrenching sobs shook her. The sounds pierced through the mansion and reverberated through the corridors and halls. A faint dull noise from some corner of her room was heard. Nili looked up and saw nothing. She fell on the bed and cried herself to sleep.

Sundays now became useless. The only day when Nili used to venture outside, ambling along with a shopping bag to the market. Haggling was hateful to her. She paid without a word, even though she knew she was cheated. Nili was a prized customer who communicated in monosyllables. Eager eyes played on her back and whispers floated along with the smell of scaled fish, to which she never gave attention. She recoiled at the touch of the shopkeepers when she paid them. Taking out her handkerchief she vigorously rubbed off the faintest trace of sensation as if she was erasing the memory of an unavoidable sin. People tore her apart when she left.

'Stuck- up bitch, that woman. High and mighty me !'

'Good customer though. Look at some of these women, haggling as if their whole life depended on a piece of coin!'

'But always the Sen pride. Treats us like dirt!'

'Poor thing! Lost her mother when she was a child. Had to run a family and look after an invalid father.'

'Too ugly for anyone to marry her. How old she looks now! How she lives alone in that old house I wonder.'

'I've heard she practises witchcraft. People are scared to go near the house after dark.'

'Haven't you anything better to do than criticising an old woman only because she keeps to herself?'

'Look what we have here. A big fan of hers. Had a secret rendezvous, I bet.'

'Shut up you bastards! Tearing up a dignified old lady to pieces just because she doesn't jabber and flirt with you like other women only to save a paisa. Shame on you, you cowards!'

Nili didn't know that there were a couple dissenting voices amongst the scandalmongers in the market, who spoke up for her. Not that she cared the least. Days passed and she let Sundays drop from memory. Often she did not cook and let do with the meagre and shrivelled fruits from the emaciated garden. Then gradually she skipped breakfast and dinner and started having a single meal. Weary and weak, she often felt too sluggish to leave her room, staring fascinated at a crack that extended from one end of the ceiling to another. She gradually fell into a stupor, while dust accumulated in the rooms, corridors and halls of her beloved house.

One day, a letter arrived. It was from a classmate, who was once very attached to Nili. Dipa had often been in her house as a child, where she was always welcome. At sixteen, she was married and soon left for the UK, where her husband worked. After Dipa left Purulia, there wasn't any communication between the two. The letter reminded Nili of her childhood and her heart was swept with indefinable sensations. Dipa and her husband Deb were leaving the UK for good and were to settle permanently in their ancestral home in Calcutta where the latter had found a job. Since there was a lot of time on their hands, Dipa suggested that they visit Purulia where she once lived.

Her parents were dead and the house was sold out. She longed to see her childhood friend before her husband settled down in Calcutta. Nili wrote promptly, inviting them to her mansion. They were to spend at least a fortnight with her. A sudden elation and energy gripped her, and as the day of arrival drew near, she briskly started working, to put the house in order.

One morning just before the day of Dipa's arrival, she discovered the mask from the rear depths of the cupboard. It was almost unrecognisable, bruised by the oblivious dust of decades. A strange metamorphosis occurred when she cleaned it thoroughly and the diabolical visage was gradually resurrected. A certain joy, a phenomenal up thrust of the 'other' ; the irresistible, unfathomable and unidentifiable 'something' captured her psychic passage. Nili, after all the decades of vacuity, at last recognised the face that tormented her in her dreams. The very face, the magnetic eyes that once captivated her as a child and

all the lost remembrances rushed through, flooding her. Nili put the mask on top of the cupboard, from where she could see it. The eyes- the mesmerising eyes held her captive.

The next day, Dipa and Deb arrived. The women hugged each other ardently. Even after forty, Dipa was still beautiful, and with Deb by her side, they looked tailor-made for each other. They brought gifts for Nili which warmed her heart. The couple was childless. Living abroad for many years they often forgot to maintain the rural properties, and hugged and kissed each other in front of Nili. Nili avoided those moments with an excuse. She served delicious meals with her meagre resources. They gossiped, the threesome, about their own lives, specially the ladies; lighting up the cinders of half forgotten childhood days. Nili refused household help and offers of shopping (which again became regular) and did everything to please her friend and her husband. Days elapsed. The couple was overwhelmed with happiness by Nili's hospitality.

Every night they retired to the east wing of the house, which was mammoth strong. A bedroom at the far end was made ready for them. Nili didn't feel tired even after the whole days' labour. Staring at the mask gave her strength and unmentionable sensations. With a candle she moved along, drawing strange shadows on the corridor walls which led to Dipa's bedroom. There were sounds that told stories of love and desire. Nili's eyes then grew fierce, nostrils twitched, her body becoming tense. She went back to her room and looked at the mask. There was fire and water inside her. Then determinedly she said to herself,

'No. No. Never.'

In the morning she went to the market. Her friend was angry.

'Nili, why don't you let us go shopping?'

'You really needn't bother about it, just enjoy yourselves', was the reply. It was her house and she was the mistress, thought Nili.

'Then we must go back to Calcutta tomorrow.'

'You certainly shall not. I forbid it.' There was something singular in Nili's voice which prevented Dipa from being importunate.

'She must have her own reasons,' Dipa surmised. There was a tinge of pity for her frail, helpless, old playmate.

Meanwhile the regular shopping of the surly old woman created ripples in the market. It was a rickshaw- puller who had brought the visitors to the huge mansion who unveiled the secret of Nili's regular shop-hopping. The shop- keepers were exhilarated!

'Let her have plenty of visitors.'

'Yes it's the time to make some money.'

They laughed behind her back but behaved with her deferentially. None of them dared to make queries to appease their curiosity. Nor did anyone go and take a look at the new inmates of the house. They were too intimidated by her and left her alone with them.

One day Deb and Dipa went for a tour of Purulia. They rented a rickshaw and left. Nili was alone in her room. Automatically Nili's eyes roved and halted on the top of the cupboard. She sat there for a few minutes as if in a trance—immobile. Then suddenly, she stood up as if in a daze and went to the shed. Taking a hammer and a gimlet she walked like a screwed- up automaton wired for a gun toting feat. Half an hour later on Dipa's bedroom door was discernible a hole, through which the whole room could be viewed. Satisfied, she went back to her room and stared at the crack on the ceiling with a strange anticipation.

Nili greeted her friends with a huge smile so rare for her, when they returned. Dipa was surprised to see the bony almost ugly face light up with delight. Afternoon was quietly turning to purple when the couple, too tired after the whole day's tour, retired to take some rest. The door closed. Inside their bedroom was a hide - and -seek of pink and yellow. Nili locked her eyes inside the gaping circle she created. Her face stiffened, hands trembled, knees quaked, but she looked on and on, sucking in the scene, the hair on her skeletal hands bristling with a vicarious sensation. At last it was over and the bedroom melted into darkness.

It was a sultry day. The heat was oppressive. Streets were bare and a few people who could not avoid going outside were seen hurrying fast to get indoors before the heat became unbearable. Shops were partially closed or awnings spread out to ward off the searing heat. Soon it swirled around the town, a prelude to the coming storm. Around three in the afternoon the sultriness increased and the air became still and suffocating. Sensing the lull to be the usual nor'wester, people did not take chances and headed home as fast as they could.

Anticipating a drenched evening, Nili went to the kitchen to prepare khichuri (a delicacy savoured specially during rainy days) which was Dipa's favourite dish. Refreshed by the break, she volunteered to help Nili but was sent back to her husband. Distressed, she complained, 'Nili why do you send me away when I have come specially to spend my time with you after so many years?'

'No darling, your husband may feel left out.'

'Who bothers? I want to talk to you!'

'Yes dear, of course. I'll come as soon as I've finished the chicken curry.'

'Who told you to take such pains for us?'

'It's my pleasure. I live alone and after so many years I have found my only friend and her husband for whom it's a delight to cook.' Dipa stopped arguing.

'Ok, but please hurry!'

She left; her eyes moist, touched by the affection of her friend.

By eight thirty, a tempest was brewing; the rumble extending from the outskirts to the heart of the town itself. It swept through within five minutes, leaving death and destruction in its wake. Trees were uprooted with electrifying speed, roofs toppled by the unbridled rage of the whirling wind that scattered dust and grime along its way. Meanwhile Nili dined with her friends. It was an excellent dinner. The conversation was energetic and inevitably turned nostalgic. Yet in spite of their enthusiasm the couple felt unusually sleepy after the wonderful meal and decided to retire early. They were terrified by the menacing blast of the storm and requested Nili to come to the eastern wing of the house where there was a bedroom, since the southern part of the mansion was almost dilapidated. But no amount of logic or reason could deter her from retiring to her own chamber. It seemed weird to Dipa and Deb who felt greatly concerned about Nili's unreasonable attitude. Not that it was unusual, considering the lonely life she lived inside the creepy old mansion which she staunchly refused to leave. Persuasion was useless. Then weighed down by uncontrollable sleep the couple stopped arguing with Nili and went to bed. The rampage of wind and water went on unabated throughout the night. Terror ran inside houses of the people who apprehended insuperable losses of life and property. The storm was not the usual nor'wester that people welcomed during summer. Its apparently innocuous start contradicted the outcome that transformed the lives of the unsuspecting villagers. Then an unexpectedly bright day signalled the end of the terrifying devastation, unveiling the spectacle of ruin and death. Frightened, dejected crowds gathered here and there to gauge the comprehensiveness of the carnage and estimate the losses incurred by it.

It was about eleven-o'clock in the morning when a boy ran to the market place where the villagers had gathered, to discuss the night's disaster. Breathless and pale he screamed at the startled group.

'The house, the huge house near the rice field has collapsed'

'What?'

'I went there and saw it myself'

'Don't play pranks boy, how can such a big house collapse?'

'May be he's right. The house was dilapidated alright.'

'Perhaps—but the woman!'

'The woman! The woman!' They cried in unison.

The southern wing of the house had crumbled. The rest of the mansion stood tall, a mute witness to the wreck surrounding it. The rubble was extensive. The bedrooms had caved in. On a cluster of wooden planks amidst the brick heap, was where they found her body. There was no sign of a wound anywhere. She lay as if in a sleep, serene and happy.

'Poor thing,' said the villagers.

The eastern side of the house was massive and rooted to the ground. The men combed that part which strongly resisted the blast. A bedroom in the far end of the corridor was untouched. The door was locked from the inside. After several loud knocks there wasn't any response. They had to break in. A couple lay on the bed. There was a faint stench. The villagers went inside. A man and woman. Stone- dead. At least ten to twelve hours ago, they guessed. Suddenly a boy screamed. On the dressing table was a mask with a smile on its lips.

Short Story by
Dante Villanueva Aguilar

Taking Chances

Just like every ordinary days, the queue at the MRT station is super blockbuster. Everyone is rushing home and the fastest way is through the mass rapid transit traversing the 56 kilometers stretch of EDSA. Arriane has to huddle to get a ride from Ayala to the last station in Pasay Rotonda. During rush hour expect the heavy foot traffic of commuters wanting to take the mrt ride just to be able to avoid the never ending traffic of EDSA.

Arriane can also opt for a cab or an aircon bus ride for ease of comfort, but she prefers the MRT going home despite the long lines and the agony of waiting for the train to arrive. She had been doing this for almost two years. Not that she wants to save for transportation expenses but simply because she was trying to bring back some memories.

She first met James at the train station four years ago. James is a very special persona who was able to tame her restless heart. As Advertising Executive in a reputable advertising company in Makati the casual relationship is no longer a serious thing, but just a part of ordinary trade. She treats every relationship with benefit and she is good at it. She just danced to the tune maybe because of the many instances that she loved and was hurt, used and abused. Yet despite the experience, she is still taking chances to love in the hope to be loved also.

Her first encounter with James was in a very awkward and hilarious situation. She was going home exhausted of the days work and on her way out of the station her attention was caught by this young man rushing to take the last trip of the train. There was that unexplained feeling she felt for the very frist instance she took a glance at the innocent but gentle aura of James.

She imagined as if thunder, lightning, storm and earthquake all happened at the same time. As if the world stood still, enough for her to get stunned. Only then she realized that she is not wonder woman when she intentionally bumped into the muscular and sculpted like body of James.

She fell flat on the floor and everyone was in great surprise looking at her. To save herself from shame, she acted as if severly hurt and about to faint. That prove to be effective enough to cause commotion particularly to James who was so worried of the situation.

"Maam, are you Okay? Please tell me your okay." rattled and restless, James supported Arriane to get up.

As if a major winner in a beauty contest at that very moment, Arriane feels like being crowned the most coveted title with James as her priced prize. They ended up at the nearby restaurant due to her insistence. James had no recourse but to give in being worried of her situation.

James is only 20 years old, half her age. He is a self supporting computer engineering student who works as a service crew in a 24/7 coffee shop in Ortigas. He was in a hurry to catch the last trip in the hope to report to his night shift duty but had to ask for an emergency leave given the incident. Arriane was somehow guilty that she offered money to compensate for the day's leave for which the latter refused.

James lives with his grandmother Lola Soleng when both of her parents separated at his young age. James talks so much about his life to the amazement of Arriane who is smitten of the guy's sincerity and innocence. His narrowed eyes, bedimpled smile while talking all add up to his charm.

They almost lost track of time as she attentiverly listens to the narrative of James. His story, even simple was interesting for Arriane to hear. James was just so engross to share his ambitions and everything he wants for his Lola Soleng which endeared Arriane's heart. Instantly there was that sparkling connections between the two of them. They have so many similar interests like watching wrestling on tv, listening to folk rock music and volleyball as sport. James was even so proud being a varsity volleyball player at school as wing spiker. The commonality makes them become comfortable with each other even for the short period of time. James was amused when she handed her calling card before they parted ways.

"In case of emergency, just call a friend."

A week, a month, two months and 3 days she had waited until she got a call from James. Lola Soleng was hospitalized due to pneumonia and was in a critical condition for a week already considrering her old age. Despite her hectic schedule for the day, she did not hesitate to rush to the hospital. It may not be proper, but she is thankful for the incident as this was the reason that James was able to communicate to her.

James was outside the ICU, anxious and restless going back and forth. Upon seeing her, he hurriedly approached Arriane and like a child wanting for protection he embraced her tightly. Arriane could feel the sigh of relief on James with her presence. She sense that so much love and concern of James to her grandmother who is in a critical situation. She can't help but cry due to mixture of pity, admiration and for sure a blossoming love for the guy . Arriane made sure that all the expenses from the hospital confinement were fully paid until Lola Soleng was discharged from the hospital.

"So grateful for the help Maam Arriane. If not for you grandma

would not survive the situation. Don't worry shall pay in installment, thats a promise" reluctant but James was so assuring and sincere in his promise.

"You owe me nothing. Its an offer for help so you are not obliged to pay."

"No please. This is too much for you. I still insist to pay."

"Can't you understand? Am extending help not a loan" gushes Arriane feeling a little bit irritated already.

"Please don't be mad, but I insist that I owe you one and shall need to pay you."

"Okay, can you pay me now, as in now?" (feeling furious) Arriane replied with a sarcastic voice.

"Are you serious? Have I not told you that shall pay, but just give me ample time. Shall pay it on installment if okay with you?"

"Precisely dear the reason that I insist that you don't owe a penny. For everything I did was an honest intention to help.End of discussion, is that clear?" Arriane feeling pissed off already.

James intended to explain further but Arriane was quick enough to ignore him, placing her fingers to his mouth to prevent him from talking. James was surprised and his reaction was funny enough for both of them to burst into laughter..

James had actually sought help from his friends and had requested for cash advance in their office. However, the money he was able to raise was not enough given the series of tests and medicine prescribed that need to be purchased. Although shy and uncertain James took the risk of calling her for the much needed help since he took hold of her last reminder when she handed him her card and said in case of emergency,call a friend. Arriane can't help but amused of the innocent but honest confession of James.

Arriane's visit to James place became frequent. She would bring some groceries for James and Lola Soleng and would sometimes stay over the weekend, cook some food and jams with James as they enjoy the videoke challenge singing out loud with their favorite folk rock music. Both have lovely voice and they blended well. Lola Soleng was also very accommodating for she treats Arriane as a new member of the family. Arriane fondly listens to James stories, hollow or corny, she finds it very sincere, no pretentions.

Each morning she is greeted with a morning message from James. A simple hello, how are you doing ? or stay safe on your way home are messages enough to melt her heart. She is starting to fall for James. Awkward as it may seem given their 20 years age gap and their status. She is not bothered even if sometimes they caught other's attention.James is not even intimated nor bothered, so why should she ? She learned to shrug it off when sometimes they are mistaken as mother and son and she at times play along with it.

In some instances that Carla is at James place, this brings discomfort to Arriane. Most often she is ignored by Carla who would always be extra sweet and caring to James as if reminding Arriane that James is Carla's property. So as to avoid friction, she would always be the first to leave for she can't stand being with the company of Carla. If not for James she would get even to Carla, but she always holds her temper for she knows she is at the losing end.

When James was hospitalized due to over fatigue, Arriane wasted no time to be at James sick bed taking care of him. Carla happened to on an out of town trip and it was a blessing in disguise for Arriane as she had all the time to be with James. Lola Soleng with her old age can no longer sustain staying at the hospital.

"Look at you. You are no superhuman ! And how many times did I remind you to always prioritize your health?"

"So sorry. I know this is much of a hussle to you. But I grreatly appreciate your time, don't worry shall make it up with youy." utters James.

Arriane pinched the nose of the surprised James. James also retaliates. They wrestle with each other until they both fall on the floor. James was over Arriane. The moment their bodies stayed close to each was a deafening silence and they hear the beating of their hearts as if gasping for air. They both looked at each other and suddenly silence engulfed the two of them.

As if awaken from a deep sleep, James rose up feeling so ashamed of himself and went back to his hospital bed. Still in silence, Arriane just casually picked up the pillows scaterred on the floor and returned it to James. James held Arriane's hands. Like a gentle sheep, Arriane became submissive to the advances of James. At that very moment she feels like a slave willing to do whatever his master commands.

She is a willing victim who will do everything to please James. His gentle caress, his moaning, his audacious tongue exploring every delicate part of her body gives unexplained sensation to Arriane.

"Whatever happened to us is not a debt repayment. I just want you to know that you mean so much to me." whispered James.

Still silent, Arriane attempted to get off the bed to cover her naked body. James tightly embraced her like a child so afraid to lose his prized possession. Right from there Arriane knows she can no longer escape James. While she has no expectations as to where this relationship leads to, she knows she has to deal this one step at a time. She knows James is still committed to Carla and knowing her boundaries she will not demand anything from James. When time comes that James shall be made to choose between her and Carla, no matter how painful it may be she has to bear the pain. But right now, what is important is that she is happy being with James.

"You know what, I think am falling for you" ; without batting an eyelash that James professes much to the surprise of Arriane who has to avoid the attempt of James to kiss her.

"Is it a result of your high fever, Are you sure you are OK?" asked Arriane.

"Why dont you believe me, look am serious."

"Serious condition? should I request you to be confined at the ICU?" jokes Arriane. Suddenly James becomes irritated

"Fuck me ! Am I really not worth believing ?" James' voice cracked as if a suppressed disappointment is brewing. Arriane was also quick to apologize seeing James in trantrums. Arriane feels like Julia Roberts of Pretty Woman. Trying to appease James she embraced him while apologizing.

"Still in doubt ? Everything I said is no joke."

"I don't know about you. It must the effect of antibiotics or something."

"Addicted to love perhaps. Come here and will show you how an addict loves his girl." James tighlty embraced Arriane biting her shoulder to her surprise that she shouted so loud. James covered her mouth so she will stop yeeling. They started flirting with each other.

At this point, it doesnt matter anymore if James is telling the truth or lying just to appease her. What matters most is she can feel the outmost respect of James for her and that alone suffice. There are instances that her conscience bothers her whenever she learns of the the beckering between James and Carla. James may not confrim it, but she suspects that she is at times the cause of their argument.

She cant deny the fact that she feels elated whenever James would confide to her about the extreme jealousy that Carla feels toward her. Whenever she receives sarcastic text messages from Carla, she just shrugs it off. She understands where the emotions of Carla is coming from.

Yes she is hurt whenever she is accused of being a relations wrecker. That she needs to find a lover of her age and not a cradle snatcher. So many instances that she attempted to avoid James, but everythime he pleads for consideration she feels so helpless, so vulnerable to the supplication of James. Call it a Motherly figure and not true love but she admits she takes advantage of the feelings of James towards her. She knows she cannot afford to leave and just forget James who means the world to her.

So as to avoid further conflict, she distanced herself to James and to Lola Soleng. During special ocassions like bithdays that she can't refuse the invitation of Lola Soleng she graces the event either earlier or very late so as to avoid Carla. They don't talk to each other and this will just spoil the celebration. While she feels ecstatic to be with James most of the time, she contends herself waiting for his availability. The other woman be like.

Coming from an overtime, she was surprised of a visit of James to her condo. It was too late at night, but he waited. His angelic face seems disturbed and distressed.

"What's up ? Any problem?" James just nodded his head. Not looking at her as if he is timid to tell of something. Arriane sat besides him.

"You may want to share with what 's inside you. I can be of help."

Still silent, Arriane taps James shoulder.

"Hello anybody home? A penny for your thought" quips Arriane.

"Carla is pregnant. She wants us to relocate to her province. I dont have the choice but to concede or I will not longer see my baby"seriously explained James with a hoarse voice keeping his emotion not to cry Arriane felt dumbfounded at that very instance. As if a cold pail of water was splashed all over her that she seemed stunned and frozen out of surprise.

"We shall leave next week as soon as I get my clearance from my company. Lola Soleng sent word of thanks to you. She will miss you and so do I."

No longer able to hold her emotion, Arriane started to cy in silence. She can't find any word to muster. A mixed feeling of grief and confusion suddenly engulfed her. She can't take her eyes off to the innocent and lovely face of the man she deeply loved. As if wanting some help, Arriane looked at her assistant who is looking at her with sad eyes. There was that timid smile from her assistant assuring her that everything shall be okay.

"Hope you will not harbor any ill feeling towards me and Carla. I know you understand the situation. Promise if given the chance shall visit you. I want to personally thank you for all the goodness you extended to me and my family. That means a lot to me and forever am grateful. Promise me you'll take care of yourself when am gone."bitterly utters James tightly embracing Arriane who is still at a loss of what is happening.

James has been gone for a long time, but Arriane remains speechless, quietly sobbing. She cried out loud when her assistant approached and hugged to console her. Arriane feels that she is alone again. As if that pain caused by the tragic deaths of her parents once again haunted her. But the pain she is experiencing right now seems too hard to bear. When these two important people – James and Lola Soleng moved away, she no longer knows how to start anew. She just feels being abandoned.

She had to take an emergency leave for a week trying to digest everything. Most of the time she spends her day melancholy watching the setting of the sun along Roxas Boulevard. Each sunset brings her mixed feeling of joy reliving those precious moments with James and pain living with those memories.

Here at the boulevard she is free to cry, to unload that sadness in her heart. She stays here until dark and decides to go home when she feels tired to be able to take a sleep and would no longer be bothered. If only her life is translated into a movie, she will handily win the best actress plum for her emote to death moments.

So much has changed in her life when James left. She decided to move out from her condo and transferred to a smaller condo together with her assistant. She has also changed her contact number and only keep in her phonebook important numbers of friends including James. She now limits nightlife with acquantancies only if it is on business matters. No more gyrating and seducing of men who are only after sexual pleasures. At this point she is not yet ready for any commitment. From work she goes straight to her condo watching tv or just simply listening to music while silently looking at the skyline from her balcony .

It has been a year that her life seems routinary. She can't deny that there are still moments that she can't help but think of Lola Soleng, most especially of James. Those precious moments that James would drop by her office to fetch her late at night. His being stubborn everytime he stays at her office keeping everything away from her, put off the aircon, the lights and her personal computer so she had to pack up her things to go home..Arriane had no choice but to heed to James insistence for her to go home and rest instead of spending the night at the office just to finish the pending works. James would always remind her to take care of herself and never be overworked to avoid being sick. It has been two years that she has not heard of James and Lola Soleng.

"Maam someboby is looking for you. According to her she is your personal friend, Carla." Said the assistant.

To her surprise, Carla was right at the doorfront, looking at her in so much anguish. Arriane suddenly felt a mixed emotion of worry and wonder seeing the woman whom she considers her rival for James' affection.

"Been looking for you since last week. I visited your last address, but was informed that you had transferred a long time ago and no one knows your whereabout. I was just so desperate looking for you until I took chances at the social media."explained Carla.

"I don't understand?" Arriane still clueless. Fear engulf her when Carla started to cry.

"James is at the ICU. It's been a month already. Lola Soleng asked me if you can possibly visit him even for the last time."

In between sobs, Carla narrated that one fateful day when they wanted to surprise Arriane during her last birthday only to find out that she already vacated her condo unit. James was so devastated when they went back to the province together with her and their son Tristan. Then along the road there was a hold up inside the bus. James had to cover them when there was a commotion as one passenger resisted. Gunfires were heard and a stray bullet hit James head. He was critical for several days as the bullet fatally hit the brain. An operation was not recommended as this shall cause the patient to be comatosed.

Arriane trembles in fear upon hearing the news. She can't help crying so loud enough for her assistant to appease her. Carla approached and embraced her and both were crying.

At the hospital, Arriane was holding her emotion so as not to cry. She was hesistant at first to enter the ICU for she is not sure how she feels seeing James. She doesn't want to see James at his sickbed like a living dead. A sobbing Lola Soleng approached and embraced her. Arriane could no longer hold her emotion that she once again burst into tears, embracing the old woman she longed.

"He has been waiting for you for so long.. Everytime I mention your name his eyes move. He may not be able to open his eyes, but the tears are manifestation that he wanted to see you.. Thank you for coming over. I know James will be glad hearing your voice" narrated a sobbing Lola Soleng.

Still reluctant, Arriane approached James' sickbed. So much has changed of James. The angelic face has suddenly matured, perhaps because of the responsibility of being a family man at an early age. She feels sorry upon learning that James was not able to finish his studies just to prioritize his being being a father, a husband and a grandson.

Arriane held James hands.He twitched. For a moment Arriane startled, looking at Carla. Carla with a sad smile just nodded her head assuring Arriane of her consent.

"James, this is Arriane. I know you hear me. Am sorry for everything. I know I had been unfair to you and to your family. I was away not because I was mad at you or to anybody. I just wanted a space to move on, to forget the pain and start a new life. It was so selfish of me. Then and now you were the only person so dear to me even if I know I was wrong all along. I just want you to know that all those years I wished only the best for both of you. You had been extra special to me and had cherished those precious memories spent with you and Lola Soleng. I asked for your forgiveness if I may have hurt you. Rest now James, I know you've struggled hard and I know you are so tired in your fight and you deserve to rest."

Tears started to fall on Arriane's eyes. Lola Soleng approached James sickbed and also held his grandson's hands. Carla was just from a distance.

"James, my child, Arriane is right, rest now your weary body. Don't worry about us, we can manage. I know it hurts me to let you go, but it will be more hurting seeing you in suffering. I know you are so tired, sleep now my child."

Tears fell on James eyes. He smiled. Arriane and Carla looked at each other seeing the monitor suddenly flatten. Carla cried out so loud and embraced his partner James. Arraine just tighlty embraced the crying Lola Soleng to console her.

At the funeral, Arriane was jus from a distance sadly watching James coffin. She remained afar until the funeral was over. She wanted it this way to allow Carla and Lola Soleng to mourn. She also wanted to mourn alone away from the scrutiny of the bystanders and other mourners.

When everybody left the area and only Carla and Lola Soleng were there, Arriane decided to come near James' tomb. At Carla's side is a little boy with James semblance. The little boy smiled upon seeing her

"Tita Arriane, how are you?"exclaimed the little boy feeling excited Arriane feeling astonished looked at Carla.

"This is Tristan, your godson. And the little baby am conceiving right now shall also be your goddaughter as this is James wish. James and Lola Soleng would always tell Tristan stories about you. Our picture during Lola Solengs last birthday is dispayed at our living area, the reason why Tristan is familiar of you."

Arriane was so speechles. She can't find a word to express how she feels at that very moment. The only thing she did was to embrace Tristan who also embraced her tightly. Arriane sat besides Carla in front of James tomb. Lola Soleng fetched Tristan away from them so the two could have time to talk.

"James would always tell me things about you. Your goodness and kindness to him and Lola Soleng. Your unconditional love especially during their down moments was extraordinary.. I admit I was so jealous of you coz you got the big share of their attention and love. It was my decision that we have to live away from you. I may have succeeded separating the three of you, but deep in Lola Soleng and James heart they have that special space for you and I know I can never replace you."

Arriane just remained silent as she continues to cry. Carla handed her a small box. Arrtiane was clueless what's inside the box. She unwrapped it to find out the tokens she gave James on several ocassions. The old photos of her and James, with Lola Soleng. She looked at Carla awaiting for an explanation.

"I saw that in James personal belongings. Lola Soleng and I agreed that the only person who can keep that is you.May that serves as memories for the the man we both loved." Carla started to cry.

"My sincerest apology if I caused the separation of both of you. I was just so much in love of James why I became so selfish, so greedy. I was too afraid loosing James. Perhaps because I know he will choose you over me. I know you are a nice person because James and Lola Soleng endears you so much and I admit I feel so jealous of you. Now that James is gone

I hope you will forgive me." Full of humility that Carla confessed.

Arriane without any remorse just held Carla's hands. At this very moment any wall that separates the two of them has been completely shattered into pieces. Whatever ill feeling they felt for each other before has now turned into understanding. They both know that this is the start of a new friendship.

"I hope you will allow me to help Tristan and your future baby girl for the sake of James memory. Thank you for taking care of James and of Lola Soleng. You have a pure heart, the reason why James chose you over me.Can I visit you and Lola Soleng once in a while?." Shyly asked Arriane.

With a smile, Carla nodded her head. They embraced each other tightly.

"Maam, it's already the last station." a gentle tap from the MRT guard was enough to awaken Arriane. Without her knowing it she fell asleep in the middle of her travel.

It's been almost two years that James has already been gone. Her one true love. The man who taught her the meaning of unconditional love – its fullness and kindness. A love that knows no boundaries, no conditions, no restrictions.Yes she can no longer relive those precious moments, but she still reminisces those memories kept in her heart.

Arriane quickly fixes herself before alighting the train. She cares less being the last passenger inside and a lot of passengers are awaiting outside for her to come out so they can board the train..

Right next to her alighting the train was the guard on duty who has just finished the inspection before allowing the waiting passengers rushing inside to get a seat. She noticed that the guard was somehow cute with a slight semblance of James. She smiled at the guard who was timid enough to return the smile.

There was that unexplained emotion she felt when their eyes met. She slowed down with her steps so the guard can walk beside her as they approach the escalator up to the exit area.

"Thank for the tap, I'm Arriane and you?"

"Ryan. I thought you were snobbish. I was wrong. I often see you taking the train, but you just ignored my greeting. Guess tonight is just my lucky night finally having your name ".

Arriane just smiled. She took her calling card and handed it to Ryan with a seductive smile.

"In case of emergency, just call a friend."

Arriane walks ahead with a smile on her face. She feels like being crowned as the 5th Ms. Universe representing Philippines coz she feels like a big winner tonight seeing Ryan's titilating reaction still being mesmerized looking at her..

Here at MRT, she realized that it's now time to move on and start a new lease of life. She wants to open doors to love again. This time around, she expects nothing from Ryan. She just wants to try to love once more, no expectations, no conditions. She is no longer afraid of taking risk to love and be hurt, to love some more and be hurt some more. In taking chances, she knows this shall be a start to start a new beginning.

Short Story by Kuntala Bhattacharya

A Retrospection

I glanced at my watch. It was 5:30 PM.

The perfect time to watch the sun setting beyond the horizon and spreading across a golden hue. I was just in time at the Princep Ghat, one of my favorite places in Kolkata. The city where I was born but could not spend my childhood. Regrets brushed aside, now I am in "The City of Joy" with a family and a home.

I trudged along the steps of the ghat, cautious of the slipperiness here and there. The rains the day before were too rough and the heavy downpour had left many areas a bit murky and soiled. It may seem insane why am I rushing to be at the ghats when it's too risky out there?

There indeed is a secret!

The bright blue sky above, the reflection of the sun rays on the Ganges, the sprawling Vivekananda Setu, the row of boats lined at the banks of the river, and the freshness in the air amplify zillions of times after the rains at the Princep ghat. The bountiful feeling within me unleashes at the sight of this magnanimous beauty. My heart and mind seek such a space, a divine opportunity to transport into a celestial world where I dwell in peace.

And so, I found a silent corner and sat down to bedazzle myself with the intrinsic beauty of nature. The faint tunes of a popular Rabindra Sangeet comforted my ears and I closed my eyes to appease myself.

"Gharete bhromor elo gunginiye

Aamare kaar katha se jay shuniye"

(A honeybee has entered inside my house humming along and transmitting information about someone unknown)

A Flash of memories from years back returned; a small girl who used to await every year for the summer vacations and the Puja vacations to visit Kolkata at her grandparent's house. A mansion of the yesteryears with artistic glamour, opulent décor, palatial aura, and an affluent taste. Yet upholding the traditional and ancient heritage of the past.

"Yes, my princess has arrived. Come on, play the conch and beat the drums." The words of my grandfather, the moment he used to spot me at the gates of the house. And then the sounds of the conch and the smiling face of my grandmother. In the next few minutes, I am into their laps, chattering and babbling in glory about my feats at school, with friends, and my extracurricular activities. Two inquisitive pairs of ears lovingly listening to each one of my words and coaxing me with warmth and affection.

I could feel tears dripping down from my eyes. How did I miss them? Their words, their touch, their smile, and most importantly their selfless love.

"Nawab Nandini, wake up? How long will you sleep?" and then the laughter of my grandfather, trying to wake me up every morning.

"Allow her to sleep. She has come to spend her vacation with us. Why do you have to wake her up so early?" my grandmother protested every time my grandfather attempted to wake me up.

The sweet fights between them were adorable. It never lasted long as my giggles interrupted them, engrossing them with my tantrums.

One of the best memories I have still engraved in my heart was when I first tried on jeans. They were super excited to watch me decked up and style on. I remember them exclaiming in joy at the sight of me.

"Oh, my little princess is looking so smart and adorable!! Come let me hug you tight, my cute baby". The words of my granny still ring through my ears like a melody.

The Puja vacations were spent fabulously, running all around the mansion, dressing up in colorful attires, attending the Puja rituals, tapping with the rhythmic beats of the *Dhaak*, chiming in with the devotional songs, and shaking my legs for the *Dhunuchi naach*. A completely toxic experience and I seldom felt like retrieving myself from the trance.

The special attraction was to wear a saree at *Ashtami* and rush for the *Anjali*.

"Rinki, stay calm. How will I drape the saree if you keep on moving like a swinging pendulum?" Every time my mother had to struggle to wrap the saree around me as I lacked the patience of standing still for a long time. And over and above that, I especially enjoyed the company of my cousin sisters and brothers and hence was always in a hurry to join them, the moment I woke up in the morning.

And then the words of my grandfather. "Who is this lady? Where has she come from? I don't think I have ever seen her before. She is so pretty and beautiful."

"Oh, come on *Dadu*, it's me Rinki."

"When did you grow up, Rinki? Now I am in a big problem. I have to search for a handsome groom for you." That was the usual way my grandfather teased me whenever I was draped in a saree.

My reply was also the same every time, hearing which, he would laugh loudly.

"Dadu, please I don't want to get married. I am still your little princess, your Nawab Nandini. And I love being like that."

After 20 minutes...

I opened my eyes and glanced at my watch again. It was 5:50 PM and the sky was by then reddish in colour. Unknowingly I chimed out a few words from my heart.

"Thy vastness is hypnotizing yet magical

These blissful moments enlighten my soul

Transfixed I am glancing at your enrapturing charm

Elated, I am venturing into your world filled with surreal and calm."

"Rinki, how about a city tour today? Shall we go? Let's visit Maidan, Victoria Memorial, and Birla Planetarium." My Mama (uncle) was always enthusiastic about a tour around the city. And I was his best companion, eager to roam around. He had a white ambassador of the old days, and he loved driving it himself. I felt like a queen sitting inside the car, grand was its appearance.

My uncle had always been an idol for me, a storehouse of information and proficient in storytelling. The way he narrated engrossing facts on the milky way, the constellations, planets, and the comets were fascinating for a little girl like me. Sitting inside the planetarium and watching the cosmic and astronomical extravaganza, induced within me a feeling of how grand the city was to offer such innumerable opportunities for novices like me to learn and absorb.

Running around the Maidan with my uncle was another amusement for me. The greenery, the soothing breeze, the fun-filled surroundings, and with my favorite companion my uncle, each moment was precious to me. I loved to sing and dance around, soaking into a world of fun and excitement. The best thing about being with my uncle was the freedom granted to jump around at my will. Only his eyes were a constant vigil, while he sat and relaxed on the field.

"Didi, didi, your black tea," Chintu's voice awakened me, as I restored myself back to reality. Chintu was a small boy, selling tea with his father at a nearby shop just beside the ghat. Since I was a frequent visitor, he knew me very well and my preference for black tea. I took the teacup from him and patted him.

"How are your studies going on Chintu? I hope you are going to school regularly. It's good you are helping your father, but never miss your studies."

"Yes Didi, I am. I am using the pencil and notebooks you gave me."

"Good boy. Let me know when you need more. I will bring more pencils and notebooks for you. It's almost 6:30 PM now and I should leave. You take care and keep on studying."

I love the smile on Chintu's face, every time I meet him. An innocent smile, ever-blooming with energy. Caressing his hair, I stood up and wished him bye.

A Leisure Stroll...

The breeze whizzed past me; a tranquil feeling refreshed my entire soul. I started walking towards

Outram Ghat, another favorite place of mine in the city. And especially the Scoop always has been my next stopover, whenever I am at this place. There is something magical in the air, beckoning me always to wrap myself within its enticing charm. When I was small, the ghats were not so full of lights and were not paved well yet running along the ghats was fun. My heart leaped with joy, reminiscing the old golden days and for a minute I felt like jumping and running the way I used to in my childhood. I smiled at myself and walked inside the Scoop.

Ice-creams and french fries – even though they defy my dietary habits, they are my favorites. I ordered and went upstairs to sit in my favorite corner. The night lights were glittering near the ghat, loved the illumination on the river waters.

I looked around me. The sitting area was full, some waiting for their food and drinks, some engulfed in conversations along with their preferred ice cream and snacks. Mind reading and guessing are one of my favorite pastimes. Whether I am on a bus, train, car, flight, or even relaxing somewhere, I love observing the people around me. The facial expressions, the activities, the verbal dialogues, and their actions are very interesting to analyze. And I could never resist engaging myself in it.

The City Lights...

Darkness had descended and the city lights were shimmering in every nook and corner of the city. Standing outside the Scoop, I could feel the vibes of liveliness and spirit. Usually, I trudge back home, but somehow, I did not feel like it. My mind was bent on scouting for more, and it was all being nostalgic about old memories.

One thing I have learnt in my life is not to deceive my heart. Repenting later is not what I desire. And so, I went on to one of my desired destinations – the street food shops right in front of Victoria Memorial.

The moment I reached the stalls and gazed at the brightly lit Victoria Memorial; my mind drifted again years back. My parents had always preferred visiting museums, planetariums, national parks, historical buildings, and monuments – a rightful way to enhance my knowledge about the different facets of our country and I definitely had a special fascination for them. The Memorial was one such place, the artifacts it houses still are a great attraction.

I sometimes wonder, the city has so much to offer and so few of us are aware of it.

"Bahenji, do you want black tea or milk tea?" The voice of the roadside tea seller floated me back to the present.

"Black tea, Bhaiya."

Relaxing at the roadside wooden bench and sipping a cup of tea is bliss and I miss it anywhere I am in the world. And not just those plastic cups but the clay cup or Kulhad. There is a special aroma in those cups, irresistible and magnetic.

"Here is your tea, Bahenji. Do you want some biscuits?"

"Thank you, Bhaiya. I am quite full today, had some snacks before coming here. But thank you."

With the cup in hand, I looked up at the sky above. My love for stargazing and astronomy had been instilled within me by my uncle. And I went on reaping on the subject till date. Tracking the constellations was fun with my uncle. We used to play a small game; the person who could trace the entire constellation earned points. And sometimes for fun, we used to deliberately create an imaginary shape and try to fool each other. I smiled recollecting the incidents.

"The tea was good, Bhaiya. Here is your money. I will definitely come back to your stall next time and will recommend my friends. So, keep up your good work."

"Thank you, Bahenji. I am honored."

This is the simplicity I love and cherish and will do, always. The city has so much life and enthusiasm embedded into its core, unlimited and unparalleled.

Time – 7:30 PM...

It was time to explore my next favourite place – Park Street. The liveliness and exuberance have always been enticing, drawing me nearer the moment I am close to the place.

I always prefer to walk from Victoria Memorial to Park Street. It approximately takes 20 minutes to reach, and I love the stroll as always. And the main reason is to envelop me with the calm breeze and watch the traffic and the people around.

The tempting aroma of "Egg Rolls" greeted me, and a dash of a smile flashed through my face instilling a feeling of gusto that I cherish so much.

"Namaste Didi, how are you?"

That was the owner of the Roll Shop where I stop by every time I visit Park Street.

"I am good, Vinod. How are you? How is your business prospering? Have things changed after the pandemic?"

Vinod smiled and replied in his usual modest tone.

"All is good Didi. Food lovers are again swarming into the shop and business is slowly picking up. Shall I prepare your favorite double egg roll, Didi? And yes, I remember no chilies and no sauce."

I laughed at the way he chuckled out my preferences.

"You never forget Vinod. Do you know that's your key to alluring customers? Yes, please prepare a double egg roll for me, with no chilies and no sauce."

I laughed again as Vinod ordered his boys to prepare the roll and I sat down at one of the wooden benches near the shop. Truly indeed business was booming for him, people were flocking around the shop ordering egg rolls, chicken rolls, and Kathi rolls. Good for him as he has a family of a wife and two kids to feed.

My eggroll was ready within 10 minutes, but I decided to pay and walk along munching and relishing it.

"Ok Vinod. Thanks for the roll. I will move ahead".

I came out into the main street and stood for a while, wondering where to go next. I still had time to budge around. It was 8:15 PM and I had promised my son to return by 10:00 PM. It's almost 18 minutes by Metro from Park Street to Dumdum so if I catch the 9:00 PM Metro I will be on time.

I decided to just go for a leisure walk, nearby the Metro; not to overshoot the time. Being Friday evening, Park Street was beaming with life and energy. People were crowding near the restaurants, or just chit chatting here and there. Love the vibes, it certainly re-energizes your brain and revives the mind. The positivity radiating across the place brings in new zeal and enthusiasm.

The melodious rhythmic beats playing at the street side stalls and shops enliven the spirit further. Unknowingly I started tapping my feet slowly to the beats. The city has so much to offer and indeed mesmerizes me. The variance in its culture, interests, food, and music is enormous; a unique combination that is rare and astonishing.

The Pleasant yet Lively Stroll...

"Have I been able to unleash all your treasures

What else is concealed within you more precious

Crave to discover the unknowns

Pine to uncover the treasures"

Every time I move around the city, these words encompass me. There is invariably something new, something eccentric, something distinctive greeting me as I roam in Kolkata. I love this space of my own, discovering the city in my way, realizing the infinite richness camouflaged in its core.

Lavish cars, palatial buildings, royal families, aristocratic households, and luxurious dresses dazzle the eyes. And on the other side, footpath dwellers beg for food. I wonder how the city maintains such an equipoise – a balancing and impartial act between two varying financial stretches. Yet the city never stoops down or crouches in fear or dilemma.

Engrossed in my thoughts, I did not even realize when I had permitted my heart to be completely absorbed in the intricacies of the city. It was almost 9 PM, when I glanced at my watch, recovering from the trance I love to linger on.

I had to rush instantly towards the metro station, hence decided to gear up my walking speed. Luckily, I had my return ticket, relieved from standing behind the long queue at the busy Park Street metro station. It was 8:55 PM when I reached the platform.

"Hey, is that you, Rinki?"

A familiar voice behind my back stunned me and I turned around to check who it was.

"Shaoli, oh my God! It's been decades. How are you?"

"I am good. How are you? Where do you stay in Kolkata? I never ever thought of meeting you in my life. Those old childhood memories of Durgapur."

We hugged each other, with tears in our eyes.

"Me too, Shaoli. I miss those childhood days and the moments spent with you. I regret disconnecting with you after the 12th standard. So, anyway, where do you stay in Kolkata? I stay in Dumdum."

"Oh wow. Must be well settled in life. I still remember you as one of our brightest students in school. I am still so proud of you, Rinki."

"Oh, come on, Shaoli. Now don't embarrass me. Hey, you didn't tell me where you stay in Kolkata."

Shaoli smiled and sighed. Her expressions confused me, and I could sense something awkward.

"I don't stay here, Rinki. Just came for a short visit to our ancestral home. The city beckons me every year, so I visit once to rejuvenate myself into its freshness."

"Where do you stay then, Shaoli? I think I have lots to catch up on. Where is our ancestral home? I don't recollect well."

"It's at Shovabazar. My uncles and aunts are still there, very adorable and compassionate. Every time I visit them, their affection never reduces even an inch."

"That's great. So, we are boarding the same train and will have ample time to speak our hearts out. And of course, now that I have bumped into you, a visit to my house is a must."

I literally chuckled at the thought of chit chatting with my childhood bestie like in the olden days.

Shaoli laughed too, "Yes definitely!"

Boarding the Metro...

The digital clock at the station showed 9:00 PM and we could see the lights of the approaching metro.

"So here comes our ride", I smiled.

Evidently, in a joyous mood of reuniting after many years and oblivion of people watching us acting like kids, we grasped each other's hands just like in our school days, waiting to board the train.

Thankfully the crowd was less, and we managed to sit side by side inside the metro. The moment we settled, we rattled out each other; so much to speak and so much to share. I felt like I have not spoken for years as I poured my heart out to my childhood friend.

And then I paused.

"Enough! I have spoken too much. Now Shaoli, you tell me about your husband, your kids, your house, everything. It seems billions of years have crossed, and we have so much to talk about."

Shaoli sighed a bit, which indeed raised an alarm. But I decided not to be judgmental before hearing from her.

"I am so happy for you, Rinki. You have a good, respected job, and a good family, and more importantly you are able to pursue your passions and dreams of being in the literary world. Speaking about me and my life, it's not so bright and delightful. Yes, I was married and dreamt of a peaceful happy life with a house, family, and kids. I am a mother of a girl, true. But I could not settle for a stable relationship with my husband. Unfortunately, or fortunately, I don't know how to define it. We have been divorced for the last 3 years. Believe me, Rinki, I struggled a lot to retain the relationship, I could not. I failed in many ways and finally decided to stay apart. That's the reason for leaving the city as the memories haunt me and distract me from leading a normal life."

I was stunned, lost for words, and sadly plunged from an elated state to a state of unhappiness.

"I am so sorry, Shaoli. I believe you dear girl in every way. The only thing I want to say is, you are a strong lady and a beautiful mother. It's better to stay away from a toxic relationship than digest and suffer every day. Hey, why don't you and your daughter come over to my place? I hope she is accompanying you?"

Shaoli smiled and held my hand, "I will Rinki. My daughter is with me. She will be so happy to meet you. You don't know how relieved I feel today after sharing about my life and speaking relentlessly."

"Come on, Shaoli. We still have lots to talk about. Shovabazar is approaching, it's the next station. I didn't even realize the time. So now you return to your home and then let's talk and plan for a fun-filled day at my house."

"Yes Rinki, that's a done deal. You take care of yourself."

We exchanged our phone numbers, took some selfies, hugged each other, and wished goodbye as Shaoli stood up to detrain.

I suddenly felt a void within me, the instance I lost sight of Shaoli.

Was I so lonely till today? Am I mimicking being happy? Am I fooling my heart each day, pretending to be leading a pleasant life? The train left the station and proceeded inside the tunnel, from brightness to darkness. I suddenly felt a symbolical resemblance to my life – a wish and desire of a little girl who had imagined her life like a princess but was thrust into the harsh realities of life with its bitterness and complexities.

The train slowly emerged into brightness, approaching the next stoppage. I could feel my mind transpiring into a realization of my strength, determination, and confidence – How I had succeeded to fight the odds, how I had encountered all difficulties and emerged victorious, and how I am adamant to pursue my unfulfilled dreams.

"Jodi tor daak shune keu na ashe tabe ekla cholo re"

(If no one is beside you, then start the journey alone)

The song written by Rabindranath Tagore chimed through my heart and mind, and I grinned within myself.

Rinki, Shaoli – what's in a name? Dreams will stay, desires will stay, and struggles are never-ending, yet at the end of the day somewhere there is a light. A light of hope, a light of happiness, a light of yearning, a light of expectation, and light of fulfillment.

We just need to perceive the path to grasp the light, maneuvering our life in the correct direction. The path drawn may not be flawless and need not be, the sole motive is to be satisfied and feel accomplished.

End of the Day...

The train approached Dumdum, my destination. I descended and decided to walk down to my house. I had a few minutes to myself and wanted to drench into my thoughts, reflections, and introspections.

Ignoring the sounds of the honks, and noises, I floated my mind into a world that I had always dreamt of. A world filled with love, adoration, and with compassion.

"Shokhi bhabhona kahare bole.. shokhi jatona kahare bole

Tomra je bolo dibosho rojoni.. bhalobasha bhalobasha

Shokhi bhalobasha kare koy…she ki keboli jatonamoy"

(Do you understand emotions, do you understand the pain? People seek love day and night. But do you understand the meaning of love? Is it very painful?)

I shivered, as I deliberately went on humming the song. Human beings seek love. But how many are privileged to gain selfless and compassionate love? Am I fortunate or am I unfortunate? A dilemma and a question for which I did not have an answer. Perhaps it is not desirable to receive a perfect response. Maybe human hearts are moulded to churn the unknowns and be content with the thoughts that need not be unmasked.

I smiled. Perhaps I am doing the same. Yet sometimes, love to unearth and unveil the true me, my inherent desires, my limitless passions, and my boundless thoughts.

I glanced at my watch. It was 10:00 PM. The curtain was slowly sinking. My one day in my city, yes it's mine, was ending. A captivating feeling resides in the city, in its air, in its people, and its surroundings. Kolkata drifts my soul into a multitude of emotions, an opportunity to rediscover myself more and more.

My son greeted me as soon as I rang the doorbell.

"Mom, you are back. I have sketched Superman. Do you want to see it?"

An instant switch back to reality. I was astonished, a few minutes back I was transported to an eternal world and now I am in real life again.

I smiled again.

"Wow, yes Roni, show me."

The next 1 hour went on listening to his chit-chat, dinner, and the remaining household chores. As I lay down in my bed, the recollections of the day kept encircling me. My imagination soared high, my wishes gained momentum, my ideations earned growth and there I was planning for my next novel.

"I love you Kolkata, trust me

Your grandeur beckons me

Your charm entices me

You arouse my fancies

Awakening my intense wishes

To capture the world in my words."

Short Story by Taniya Briana

The Ultimate

Money, power, influence has always been the cause of human progress. Genius has to succumb to all this. But there are some talents who are hard to beat; this is the story of a genius who proves that talent is beyond everything. Nowadays, with the increasing number of reality shows singers, dancers and various performers from different parts of the country are appearing in front of people through different television reality shows. This story is about a singer whose is 19 years old and has just passed high school and got admission in college. Namira Kaur, her father is Punjabi and her mother is Bengali. Namira has a tall and beautiful body due to her father's genes. Namira used to sing bhajans in the Gurdwara since childhood, she learned Punjabi music from a folk guru. She has a very beautiful voice and she loves singing. Her father has two trucks, one is driven by her father and the other is rented. Though belonging to a lower middle-class family, she leads a happy life with her family. Her mother being Bengali, they also have the ability to speak Bengali at home. She especially liked Rabindra Sangeet (Rabindra Nath Tagore songs) and whenever she got a chance, she would sing Rabindra Sangeet.

Namira's guru one day forcefully sends her to an audition for a famous Indian reality musical show. After many formalities and hurdles, Namira finally got a chance to compete in that show. After this begins her most difficult testing period in her life. What she would see and think from a distance, about all these famous celebrities, now she could see them closer, all as it actually is; behind the scenes. What she saw on screen was very different from what it actually was. In order to sing, one had to learn to walk, learn to talk and even learn to dance. She didn't realise all these before but being selected in the reality show she had come to understand that without learning to dance, talk and walk her song would have gone to waste. As usual, in this competition, some lovely girls and boys of rich parents, some celebrities, students of judges have taken part. Their PR agency is working for them; promoting them, sending SMS, whatsapp and Youtube link on social media of the show for them and whatever else was required. Some agencies reach out to her family, but Namira's father does not agree and stands for her strong talent in singing. In the meantime, different kinds of mental torture start; the television channels dive into the matter of increasing their TRP because she comes from a poor family. To increase TRP more and more, they start to look at Namira's family and force them to act in different advertisements. Because her family started gaining sympathy from the audience, also simultaneously a group of competitors in the show started to oppose her in the show.

Slowly she reaches the top ten names by using only the talent of her singing. Now started another story , Various event agencies start harassing her family again. Some wanted to make a 5-year agreement in exchange of money and someone wanted to tie her to different kinds of commitment in exchange of shows. Despite pressure from various judges and other candidates Namira reached the semi-final only due to her talent. Here comes in a new problem. Now the agencies have started bargaining against her talent, they were pressuring her to bribe the judge to reach the top. Again, the brokers inside the channel said that if you spend so much money, you will reach greater heights. This is a strange world, in front of which Namira has appeared, so many temptations, so much tricks. But among all these evils there are some good people, some really good judges who do not shy away from appreciating the real qualities and they help her a lot. After all these struggles Namira wins the final with her talent. Nothing could anymore stop or suppress her. After so much she comes out victorious due to public support and poll. Immediately, she caught the eye of various music directors and they started playback singing with her.

Today Namira is a renowned singer in the world of music, she is the judge of many reality shows herself. She is a true and honest judge and only judges candidates by their true talents. The flow of talent in India has progressed and continues to progress in this way for ages. Nothing can hold back true talent.

About the Authors

Dr. Alokparna Das

A full-time journalist for almost 30 years, Dr. Alokparna Das is also a trained classical musician. She has published more than one thousand articles in newspapers and magazines, and several research papers in academic journals. Her first book, *Prominent Hindu Deities: Myths & Meanings*, found mention in the Encyclopaedia of Hinduism published by Routledge. Her second book, *Haveli Sangeet*, won the Golden Book Award and IIWA Woman Writer of the year. Her third book, *Abodes of the Sun God*, won her the Non-Fiction Author of the Year. Her first short story, "The Charioteer," was one of the winners at a national-level creative writing competition. Her short stories have been published in *Stories From India Volume II* and *Philo's Prodigy Volume II*. She has also won the Research Excellence Award for her academic writing and several prizes at music competitions.

Purnima Dixit

Purnima is a writer by heart with thoughts in mind and words on paper—inking emotions through her writings. A writer with passion for simplicity, she loves to express her emotions, experiences and opinions about anything that fascinates her. The world of writing inspires and interests her to paint pictures with words. A literature postgraduate, she has always been an avid reader, which inspired her to start writing. From simply writing reviews of a few TV episodes on WordPress, she moved to penning down fictional stories. Gradually she developed interest in writing poems. She has been writing since 2015 and desires to follow her passion. When not writing, you can find her listening to good music, reading, and most importantly watching Korean dramas.

Piyush Pratik Mohanty

Piyush Pratik Mohanty is a poet, writer and author. He's 22 years old. He belongs to a beautiful place called Joda in Odisha and currently resides in Bhubaneswar. He is pursuing his bachelor's degree in the field of Prosthetics and Orthotics. An avid reader since childhood, he loves to pen down his imagination and thoughts. He loves to cook, play tabla, and most importantly write. Writing is his zeal; it gives him energy and courage to do anything in his life.

Valerie Blue Claveria

Valerie Blue Dam-at Claveria currently resides in Karagawan, Kabugao, Apayao, Philippines. She is engaged, vivacious, bubbly and down to earth; her favorite ministry is WIN, a born soul winner and evangelist by heart. She has a degree in B.A. Communication (Journalism as concentration, minor in Broadcast Communication) from the University of the Philippines Baguio. She graduated with her Doctor of Public Administration Degree at Cagayan State University in Carig Sur, Tuguegarao City, Cagayan, Philippines in July 2022. She is the second eldest daughter of retired Colonel Binsin Pawig Claveria and Dra. Corazon Dam-at Claveria. She is a sister to the late Atty. Xandred, BJ, Vina, Dex and Angel.

Leslie Riola

Leslie is the winner of a writing contest at UP Diliman and got featured in the Global News Section of a nationwide newspaper. She's a google local guide and a freelance researcher.

Charles Tomeldan

Charles Tomeldan is a certified Life Skills and Self Discovery Coach, a certified Lean Six Sigma Yellow Belt and a writer at heart. He worked as a Freelance Writer (Professional Writing Team) on Writers.PH, and wrote articles for two I.T. lifestyle magazines: PC Shopper and PC Direct. His stories "Nine Plus One" and "The Midnight CEO" were included in the anthologies *Silent Nights and Happy Ever Afters* and *The Billionaire Story*, respectively. A bachelor to this day, Charles lives in Quezon City, Philippines.

Satabdi Saha

Satabdi is a bilingual poet and author. Her writings cover varied subjects. The major ones are against injustices in life—domestic and international. Satabdi's anger is centred around female infanticide, womens' exploitation, poverty, exploitation of children, war, terrorism in all its forms, exploitation of poor, domestic violence etc. She is spiritually and romantically inclined, writes horror stories and delves deeply into things unusual and quirky. She has received awards and certificates, published 4 books and contributed poems, articles and stories in Bengali and English. She also contributes profusely to online and printed magazines and anthologies internationally.

Dante Villanueva Aguilar

Dante is a licensed Real Estate Broker, Columnist, Novelist, Scriptwriter and Author. He is a graduate of a Bachelor of Science in Commerce major in Business Management and the only graduate of his class with Latin Honors. He is an award winning writer in English, Filipino and Hiligaynon languages. He's the 2022 FWD P100k Grand Prize winner for "Self Love Story." Dante is also the author of Amidst Serenity and One Sunset Memoir and was awarded Fiction - Emerging Author of the Year 2022 by Ukiyoto Publishing for his novel One Sunset Memoir.

Kuntala Bhattacharya

Kuntala is an IT Consultant by profession and a writer by passion. She loves to travel and meet new people. She has published 14 books in her name: (1) *A Miraculous Discovery in the Woods* (novel), (2) *The Treasures of Life* (poetry), (3) *Come and Explore India With Me* (Travel magazine), and jointly with other authors: (4) *The Indigenous Compositions*, (5) *Impromptu*, (6) *My Heart Goes On*, (7) *Wide Awake*, (8) *They are Watching Vol IV*, (9) *The Kolkata Diaries Vol II*, (10) *The Loup*, (11) *Summer Waves Vol 1*, (12) *Stories From India*, (13) *Philo's Prodigy Season 2*, and (14) *A Time For Thrills*.

Taniya Briana

Taniya Briana is an International well known personality. She is an author and educator. She is the author of three fictions- 'A Journey With You', 'A Masked Identity' and 'Behind the Curtains' and contributed her stories to anthologies like 'Wide Awake' and 'Kolkata Diaries. 'Tales in the City' is one more example that shows her love for writing.

www.ingramcontent.com/pod-product-compliance
Lightning Source LLC
LaVergne TN
LVHW041706070526
838199LV00045B/1227